What If?

By Caroline Johnston

ISBN: 978-0-9570039-0-3

For more information about Caroline Johnston, please access the author's website at: www.carolinejohnston.co.uk

Cover design: Natalie Phillips Orzame

Published by IC⁴ Publishing

Titles by Caroline Johnston

Young Adult Fiction

What If?

Why Not?

Fiction

Raincoats & Sunglasses

Dedication

I would like to thank those who helped to shape "What If?":

Cherith Baldry for her advice that helped to shape the storyline.

Ian McGregor for his encouragement and editing.

John & Eleanor Johnston for their encouragement and editing.

Natalie Phillips Orzame for designing the front cover.

Mum and dad.

And most of all for Innes, Calum, Cameron & Cara

CONTENTS

Chapter 1 – What If?

I was so nervous I could feel my heart beating faster than normal; I was sure I could feel the blood pumping through my veins at 100 miles per hour. I was shaking with excitement and anticipation. I was waiting to find out if I had a part in the school play.

I couldn't believe how nervous I felt about the whole thing, especially as I'd only decided at lunch time that I would audition for the play.

I had been having lunch with my best friends, Anna and Julie. While we had been waiting for lunch we had seen the poster announcing that auditions were being held that afternoon for the school play.

"*What If* you audition for the school play, Rachel?" asked Anna, as she read the poster. "You've been saying for ages now that you would like to try something new, and you always enjoy taking part in the drama sketches at church."

"I don't know. Can you imagine me on the school stage?" I had replied.

"Yes!" said both Anna and Julie, as if it was such an

obvious thing for me to do.

So I had turned up at the main hall after classes ready to give it a go. Neither Anna nor Julie were auditioning. Anna didn't have the time; she is in the regional swimming team, and spends a lot of time training and competing. And Julie isn't interested in drama. But as I entered the hall I was disappointed to see that there weren't that many other third year pupils in the hall. Everyone knows that most of the parts are given to fourth years and above.

I picked up a script from the table at the door and walked over to an empty chair. Sitting on my own just made me feel even more unsure and nervous of auditioning. I looked through the list of characters and read the synopsis of the play. I decided I would try for one of the smallest parts; I thought I would have a better chance of getting into the play then. The older pupils would all be going after the bigger parts; so hopefully not so many people would be trying out for the part of the character called Jemma.

Jemma didn't get to say much in the play, but the few lines she had at the end sounded quite dramatic:

""What If...?" Just two little words, but two little words that can change the world!

The Scientist asks "What If?" and a new medicine is discovered.

The Inventor asks "What If?" and a new product is presented to the world.

The Politician asks "What If?" and a country's government is improved.

But what happens when the teenager asks "What If?""

I read the words over and over to myself, waiting

for my turn to go up on stage. Should I read them out really dramatically? Should it be over acted? Or should I try and be more subtle? It was really difficult to try and decide how to pitch it. As I was thinking about the best way to deliver the lines I looked up. I couldn't believe it! Of all the third year pupils why did Fiona need to audition for the play?

Fiona is in several of my classes. It's fair to say that we don't agree on much, or get along with each other very well. She seems to love nothing more than to put me down, preferably when there is an audience. I'm never able to get the better of her. And that's the way it's been with us right from day one of high school.

On that first day, while we were all standing about in the main hall waiting to be assigned to our classes, we just happened to be standing next to each other. I noticed that her ear was damaged, with a bit of the lobe missing, I now realise this must have happened from an earring being ripped out.

Out of concern I had asked, "What happened to your ear?"

"Oh, don't be such a baby," she replied. And that's been the story of our relationship ever since.

I was brought back to the present with my name being called out by Mrs Walsh, the drama teacher. "Rachel. Rachel Anderson. You're up next."

Oh well, here we go, time to shine.

"Which part are you reading for?" asked Mrs Walsh.

"I'd like to read for the part of Jemma," I replied.

The hall fell silent as I prepared to read my lines. All of a sudden I was consumed by panic. *What If* I was so rubbish that Mrs Walsh just laughed me out of the hall? *What If* I was the worst person to try out for a part today? *What If* I wasn't as good as Fiona?

I've been in quite a few drama sketches and plays at church, so I am used to standing up on stage and acting. But standing on the school stage is a lot scarier than I thought it would be. I paused for a few seconds, took a deep breath, and said a prayer. It worked. I felt calmer. I took another deep breath and read out the lines from my script.

After my audition, the next person up was Fiona, who was also auditioning for the part of Jemma. I had to admit she did sound pretty good reading through her lines, but I would never admit that to Fiona. There was no appearance of nerves, or any kind of doubt in Fiona.

Once she had finished, Fiona walked past me to go back to her seat; as she did so she threw me a look of superiority and complete confidence, suggesting the part was as good as hers.

After Fiona there were another ten people still to audition. We had to wait for everyone to finish then Mrs Walsh, and her assistant Miss Green would decide who was getting which parts. As I waited for everyone else to finish I decided that I may as well use the time to read through the script.

The play was entitled "*What If?*" and was all about a teenager called Sally and her gal pals (Jemma is one of her pals), and potential boyfriends. Really just the general ebb and flow of teenage life and relationships. The part of Sally would be played by Claire; that had already been decided on. Not that anyone minded. Claire is amazing. She's probably the most popular girl in school and is just so nice. She's been in all the school plays since she started high school, and now she's in her final year at school, so this will be her last school play. The timing of the school play had even been changed this year to make it easier for Claire to take part. Normally the play is just before Christmas, but this year it was being held in October to keep it further away from the exam prelims.

Finally, the last person auditioned and it was time for the announcements. And so here I was, shaking with nerves, wishing that Anna or Julie was with me. I cast a quick glance back towards Fiona; I could tell she was assuming she had the part, she was sitting with such a smug look on her face.

"Rachel Anderson," oh, here goes, the moment of truth, I closed my eyes as if somehow that would help, "will be performing the part of Jemma."

What was that? I couldn't believe it! I'd been picked for the school play! And added to the sweetness of it all, I had beaten Fiona to the part. The look on her face was priceless. I wondered what explanation she would be giving to all her posh friends as to why it was me that had got the part and not her. I know you're not supposed to gloat over other people's misfortunes, but sometimes it's just hard not too, especially when it involves Fiona.

I couldn't wait to leave the drama department and tell Anna and Julie the good news. As soon as the auditions were over I went to Anna's house. It's our monthly routine. One Friday night a month Julie and I go straight to Anna's house from school and have a sleepover. We always have loads of fun.

As I got to Anna's house both Julie and Anna threw open the door with expectant looks on their faces.

"I got it!" I screamed in delight. "I'm in the play. The only third year with their own speaking part. Fiona didn't get the part, I did!" Anna and Julie pretty much have the same opinion of Fiona as I do.

They both gave me huge big hugs.

"Wow, Rachel, *What If* this is the start of your world famous acting career?"

"I hardly think so, Anna," I laughed. But still, *What If...*

Chapter 2 – David

I had such a good weekend. Friday had been so much fun, finding out I was in the play and then having the sleep over at Anna's. Saturday had been full of fun family stuff. Mum, dad, Ben, Amy (my brother and sister) and myself went 10-pin bowling then went to a restaurant for dinner. Sunday was church as usual, and then round to Anna's house for the afternoon. Fun weekends are great, but it just makes Monday mornings feel even worse than usual. Mondays are not my favourite day. The dislike for the day starts from the second the alarm clock goes off.

During the weekend you have freedom to live to your own time frame. But that alarm clock on a Monday morning is the first reminder that you are back to living your life to the time frame of school. Monday mornings are just crazy at my house. Everyone has hit the snooze button on their alarm clock once too often, and then we all rush around each other with short fuses, desperately looking for missing socks, shoes or school books. Breakfast on Monday mornings is always eaten on the run. But most weeks I do actually make it to school on time.

I walk to school with Anna on Monday and Friday mornings. The rest of the week she has her early morning swimming sessions. We have an arrangement that I text her as I'm leaving my house, and then she'll be ready outside her house by the time I get there.

"I'm so tired!" I complained to Anna. "I just hate Monday mornings. It's so hard to get out of bed."

"I know what you mean," replied Anna.

Although I have my doubts that she does know what I mean. Anna is one of those annoying people who always looks fab, even first thing in the morning. Maybe because of all her early morning swimming sessions 9am feels like she's already reached the middle of the day.

Monday morning is usually a quiet walk to school, as I'm too tired to talk. I always feel tired on Mondays, by Tuesday I'm okay, probably because I like Tuesdays. But Mondays are just hard going. Obviously the Monday tiredness is just my body's way of saying there is no point in waking up and that I should spend the day under my duvet. Today's weather wasn't making it any easier, it was miserable. Goodbye summer, hello autumn.

Amazingly we made it to school for 9am. Anna, Julie and I are in the same registration class.

Anna and I have been friends since we were babies, our parents are friends and we go to the same church. We've known Julie since we started primary school. It's funny thinking back to the start of friendships, so much of it is vague. Julie just seemed to join in with Anna and me in the school playground one day and we've been friends ever since. It amazes me we're friends, it doesn't appear that we have that much in common, for example Julie doesn't go to church, she barely believes in God, and Anna and I see way more of each other than we do of Julie. Also, Anna and I live on the same street, but Julie lives on the other side of town. She used to live a few streets away, then a couple of years ago her family moved. But still we've kept together all these years. I think Julie is a really secure person, and just doesn't feel intimidated. I wish I was like that! She told me once that she doesn't feel the need for a close, best friend.

The bell rang to signal the end of registration and the start of classes. And here we come to the next thing I dislike about Mondays. Double Maths! Who on earth thought anyone would be happy at the prospect of one and a half hours of Maths first thing on a Monday? It's just cruel. As you can tell, I'm really not a big fan of Maths. What practical good is Trigonometry going to do me? I think it's one of those things you're either good at or not. And I'm not. But despite that I ended up being put in one of the "clever" Maths classes. I think that was down to my understanding of Arithmetic rather than any detailed awareness of Mathematical equations. Arithmetic makes sense to me. I can see the point of it. It's a very useful thing to be able to add and subtract in many different aspects of life. But the rest of Maths is a challenge for me.

Thankfully Anna is in my Maths class, and, like me, does not enjoy the subject. On our first day we decided to sit up at the back of the class, as if being further away from the teacher would lessen the need for understanding. Two of our other friends, Margaret and Louise, had the exact same idea, and sat just in front of us. For the first couple of weeks it actually made for a nice class set up, until our teacher, Mr Thomson, got fed up with us chattering all through his class and split us up. So now instead of sitting next to Anna I'm sitting next to David. I must confess that this new arrangement has not provided Mr Thomson with the peace he was hoping for. Now instead of chatting with Anna, I argue with David.

I should explain a few things about David. He comes from one of the "nice" suburbs of town, and, like many of the teenagers from there, is rather full of his own importance, for no other reason than his postcode. He's not exactly in *the* cool group. But he is definitely in one of those upper social groupings.

Unlike me, David is actually good at Maths and loves to tease me when he gets higher marks than me in class tests. Now please don't get me wrong, our arguing is nothing to do with having a secret liking for each other. At the age of fourteen there only seems to be two reactions to members of the opposite sex - you either have a crush on them, or just want to hit them.

He is quite good looking, and he knows it. It's just another one of the things that he is smug and big headed about. One day in Maths class he took great delight in telling me that last Valentine's day he got ten Valentine cards. And laughed because I admitted I hadn't got any. Part of me wouldn't be surprised if he'd sent himself all ten cards.

As I sat down at my desk I accidentally hit David with my bag, which of course just set us off arguing right from the start of class. Unfortunately Mr Thomson started the class by handing out our results from last week's test.

"Perhaps if you put as much effort into studying, as you do into talking during class, Rachel, you would do better in Maths," said Mr Thomson, as he handed me my test paper.

"Yes sir," I replied, as I tried to ignore David's smug expression. I could already tell he'd got another A.

Mr Thomson is a really nice teacher, he explains things well and does seem like a nice guy. It's just unfortunate that he is a Maths teacher. The nice part of him is displayed in his role as our Guidance teacher. Despite my lack of mathematical ability, he is able to see that I am reasonably capable at other subjects.

Hey Anderson, what low score did you get this time?" smirked David.

"Oh shut up you swot."

"If you need some extra tutoring the school will be able to give you some contact details."

"And how would you know about that David? Have you needed some extra help yourself?"

"As if! Haven't you seen how good my grades are in all my subjects?"

"You're so full of yourself, you make me sick."

"You're just jealous because you need to sit next to such genius, and it just reminds you of how stupid you are."

"Do you really think that about yourself or are you on some mission to annoy me?"

"Rachel! David! If you don't mind the rest of the class is ready to start today's lesson. Stop talking and pay attention!" shouted Mr Thomson from the front of the class.

Everyone looked round at us. I felt my face flush bright red at the unwanted attention. I was annoyed that I'd allowed David's words to get to me. It's not the comments about my mathematical abilities that bother me; I just can't believe he can sit there and be so smug about his own achievements and have such a puffed up view of himself.

For the next hour I managed to ignore the annoying David and concentrated on the Trigonometry equations staring at me from the whiteboard. How could this stuff ever be relevant to my life? I ended up day dreaming about the school play. Dreaming that I would end up being the surprise star of the show.

"Wakey wakey Anderson," taunted David. "It's time for you to wake up and leave my presence for your next class. Did you stay up too late last night watching some trashy chick TV show?"

I glared at him without saying anything. David was a real challenge for me!

Chapter 3 - Hockey Sticks

"You okay?" asked Anna, later on at lunch break. "You took off so quickly from Maths class. You looked kind of upset. Are you okay?"

"It's just being in class with David."

"Come on," said Anna. "You just need some "yummy" school food inside you to cheer you up again."

Actually the school canteen isn't too bad. It really depends on how quickly your year gets served. On Mondays we are the second year group in, so you normally get quite a good selection. A few years ago there was a big shift with school dinners to provide healthier food; on the whole it does taste good. Although there are a lot of kids who go out of school to the shops to buy chips and stuff. I know my mum would be mad at me if I even thought of eating anywhere other than the school canteen.

As usual Anna was right. I felt better for my salad roll and cake. My Monday treat to myself is to buy a piece of chocolate cake. After sitting through so much Maths I owe my brain cells extra energy. Plus getting to hang out for an hour with Anna and Julie helped relax me too.

To help boost my mood, Julie decided it was time

for one of her crazy games, she makes up people watching games all the time, which usually send me into fits of the giggles. Today's game was to look around the lunch hall and decide who had put too much effort into what they were wearing that day versus who hadn't put any effort into their day's wardrobe. "And it can't just be a girls versus boys thing," Julie said explaining the rules, "it needs to go both ways. And your bonus point will come from suggesting who was dressed by their mum!" Julie said this just as I was taking a sip of cola, which resulted in me choking on it, and then the cola ended up coming down my nose. Then Julie started giggling. We knew people round about were looking at us strangely, but sometimes you really don't care what people think, you just enjoy the moment. I think it's all down to friends giving you confidence.

But after the good food and good company of lunch it was into the next negative of my Mondays - PE class. I enjoy sports and activities, but somehow school seems to take away the fun aspect of sports, and makes it boring and overly organised. Also, I'm the one that is always last to be picked for the team. I wouldn't say I was that bad at sports, but being picked for a team is more about popularity than physical ability. As I'm not part of a 'cool' group I'm down the pecking order of being chosen. Anna and Julie always get picked ahead of me. They both play for the school netball team, and so have a higher sports profile. Anna really enjoys her sports, she's quite happy to sacrifice some of her time to be on a couple of sports teams at the same time.

As the bell rang to signal the end of registration we walked over to the gym hall. Today's class is hockey. I enjoy hockey, but it's one of the sports that requires being selected by a team captain.

And here's where my week with Fiona starts.

As you'll have picked up by now, there is no love lost between Fiona and me. Also, Fiona is David's neighbour and girlfriend! She has the same inflated opinion of herself as David does. Fiona and I sit next to each other in Home Economics. And as with sitting next to David in Maths, that usually involves quite a bit of arguing.

Fiona always had an amazing ability to make me feel small, boring and insignificant. The old saying may go "Sticks and stones may break my bones but names will never hurt me." But it's really not that true when you've got a sensitive nature. Fiona seemed to know just the names, or at least the way of talking to me, to hurt. I wished I wasn't so insecure. But I just didn't know how to get tougher.

When it comes to hockey, Fiona is crazy. She wields her hockey stick like a golf club. Which usually means her team is the winning one as no one will go anywhere near her for fear of being struck by her stick. Funnily enough she's in the school hockey team, so she knows how she should play. But I think she likes to show off, or prove a point in PE. The teacher, Miss Gibbons, really likes Fiona so never mentions anything about her playing style. And that just seems to encourage Fiona to get more and more crazy.

The advantage of being last person selected meant that I was a substitute. I stood at the sidelines and watched. It was really quite cold, so it would have been nice to be able to run around. We have the most ridiculous school gym kit. Shorts, t-shirt and knee length socks. When the weather gets colder, like today, we all try and stretch our t-shirts down as far as possible, and pull our socks up as high as they can go. The worst time of year though is in January, when the temperatures are close to zero and we have to go out and run cross country wearing the same kit. We all come back with blue knees and chattering teeth.

"Rachel, Rachel Anderson," shouted Miss Gibbons. It was time to substitute one of the other girls on my team. My enthusiasm to get on the pitch was short lived when I realised that I was marking Fiona. I said a quick prayer for my survival.

I decided that the best tactic was to let Fiona stay about five metres away from me. That way there was a chance I would remain in one piece. Okay, so I'd be useless at stopping her from getting the ball, passing it on, or scoring goals. But I was sure the rest of my team would be sympathetic.

As I ran onto the pitch I was sure I could detect a smirk on Fiona's face. I definitely had to avoid her. She looked like she was planning a stick swing at me. Perhaps she was hoping to ram her hockey stick into my face so that she would then be able to take over my part in the play. I don't think they would let someone be on stage with a broken nose.

Miss Gibbons blew her whistle for the game to resume. With a pretence of enthusiasm I ran over to Fiona as if I was serious about marking her. But thankfully my prayer for protection was answered, when, after just a few passes, the fire alarm went off. Even though we were nice and safe playing outside we still needed to head over to one of the designated fire assembly points.

"Okay girls, everyone stand in line and move over to the football pitches," instructed Miss Gibbons.

Fire alarms are a fairly frequent occurrence at school. It's either from something burning in the school kitchens, the science classes, or just some pupil wanting to cause disruption to the school day.

After ten minutes the school was declared safe by the firemen. Another false alarm. There was no point in trying to get back to the game of hockey. So it was back to the changing rooms to get ready for our next class. What a relief!

After PE my last class on Mondays is Business Studies. It passed quickly enough and then finally Monday classes were over.

And now on to rehearsal. I took a deep breath as I pushed open the hall door. World of acting here I come!

Chapter 4 – First Rehearsal

I was full of excitement as I walked into the hall. But my excitement was short lived when I noticed Fiona and David were also there. No way! What were they doing here? How could it be possible that Fiona and David were in the hall waiting for rehearsals to start? Then I noticed their violin cases, I guess that means the school band is part of the play. I felt disappointed that Fiona and David were going to be part of this experience.

As I moved further into the hall I became aware of a huge buzz of anticipation. The first and second year pupils were already sitting over on the far side of the hall, full of excitement at being involved with the school play, and getting to be around some older kids. The first and second years were providing the musical input for the play, performing a few songs between acts.

I sat next to some of the fourth year pupils, many of whom had parts similar in stature to mine. I decided it would be acceptable for me to sit next to them. There was a constant hubbub of noise in the hall, with many excited conversations going on. I felt lonely. I really wished that there was someone else from my year in the play. The people around me were so busy chattering with each other they didn't notice me.

"Hi!   It's Rachel, isn't it?" asked a familiar voice beside me. "You've got the part of Jemma, haven't you? I'm Claire, just wanted to come over and say hi."

I couldn't believe that Claire had come over and talked to me. I also couldn't believe that she would feel the need to introduce herself. Of course I know who she is. Even though there are about 1,500 pupils at our high school, I think everyone knows who Claire is. And here she was talking to me. I didn't feel lonely any more, I felt like one of the most important people in the room.

"So are you excited about being in the play?" she continued.

"Yes, I really am. My friends suggested I should audition; I don't think I would have otherwise. And now I'm really looking forward to it."

"That's great. I'm sure you'll really enjoy it." And with that she walked off back to her friends. Wow, I couldn't believe that Claire had come over to speak to me. Life was certainly looking up with this acting business.

Mrs Walsh started the rehearsal by giving everyone a new script, she had made some final changes after last week's audition. It was very gratifying to see my name on the cast list, even if it was quite far down the list. I was surprised to see how many people it took to put on a play. There were a group of kids from the Art department, to help with preparing scenery. There were the kids from the school band. The first and second years for the choir sections. And those of us chosen to be actors.

Mrs Walsh was in charge; she also had Miss Green as second in command, Mr Young the band leader and Mr Smith, from the music department to lead the choir. I couldn't see how there was any way that this play was going to be pulled together in six weeks. It seemed to me that there were too many people involved, too many different factors.

"As you know, we have an ambitious schedule for this year's play. So we'll begin immediately, you may use your scripts for the first two weeks, but then after that you should all know your lines. All characters who are in the first scene up on stage now please." Mrs Walsh is not one to be put off by a challenge. She's quite a scary teacher, so people tend to do what she tells them.

I flicked through the script. There it was! My character had a line to say in the first scene. How exciting, right from the start of rehearsals I was to be up on stage!

Chapter 5 - Church

My next big *What If* came a couple of weeks later at church.

Our church has a really cool youth church. Every alternate Sunday we have our own youth meeting, rather than being in with the main church. Even our meeting room is fun. We get to use the top floor of the church hall. Mark, our youth pastor, has arranged that this area is solely for our use. It's kitted out with bean bags, a couple of couches, a football table, a bookcase full of teen books and a fridge for our cola. Once a month Mark runs a youth club for us with some of his friends. They bring their games consoles and link them up to big screens around the room. Mark will plug in his mp3 player at full volume. It's always a fun night. Although it does usually follow the pattern of boys on the games consoles, and girls hanging out on the couches chatting. It's such a stereotype, but the boys get so competitive with the games that they just don't notice that we would like to play the games too.

When we have youth church it's still pretty cool. We still get to hang out on the bean bags and couches. Mark always has different formats, so you never know what he will be doing from one meeting to the next. Mark has been our youth pastor for about a year now. He's loads of fun. He's one of those people that I would characterise as an amazing advert for Christianity. Really strong in his faith, but he lets people find things out at their own pace and doesn't force them. He's also loads of fun with a real streak of mischief about him. Personally I think his main reason for being a youth pastor is to give him an excuse to go to amusement parks and outdoor centres.

Mark is currently working through a series involving an alternative look at Jesus' life. Most of us at youth church grew up going along to church, so we're really familiar with a lot of the stories. Mark came up with the idea of the alternative bible study, to try and stop us skimming over the stories we're so familiar with, and make us stop and think more about Jesus.

Take the last time we got together as an example. We were looking at the story of Jesus and Lazarus from John chapter 11, where Jesus raises Lazarus from the dead. Mark had asked me to read out the account from the bible. As I finished reading he ordered us all to get our jackets on and told us we were going for a walk. He took us to the local cemetery, interesting outing!

"Now everyone, just imagine you were with Jesus and someone you knew had just died. Jesus brings you to the person's grave, gets the soil removed from the top of the coffin and then commands the person to come out of their coffin. How would you feel?"

"How would I feel?" I said. "You wouldn't see me for dust I would be terrified!"

"Awesome!" "Cool!" came the expressions from the boys in the group.

Still it really did get the point across. It's good to stop and think about what the Bible talks about.

As well as Anna and me, there are quite a few other kids about our age there too. Some of them are at the same high school as us, others are from further away and go to different schools. One of the boys, Andrew, is a friend of David. He is actually quite nice, not really sure why they're friends. I've kind of known Andrew forever. He grew up going along to our church too. But somehow we've never really hung out, or got to know each other that much. He hangs out with the other guys, and Anna and me just keep to ourselves. Andrew is in our year at school; he's only in my Biology class, other than that I don't see much of him. Although I will be seeing more of him for the next few weeks, as he's also in the school band and therefore at rehearsals.

Which brings us onto our challenge for this week.

"*What If* Jesus was a fourteen year old boy, living in our town, going to your school and one of your friends? What would he be like? What difference would that make to your life, and to those around you?" asked Mark.

"It's too easy to keep Jesus to some vague person who lived 2,000 years ago. So what would change if you started thinking of him as being alive now, and being in your group of friends? Try living it out over the coming month. Think of Jesus as being in your group of friends. Being in classes at school. Being in your after school activities."

Mmmm! Interesting idea. I think it sounds kind of exciting, but I'll need to discuss this one with Anna and get her thoughts on it.

On a Sunday I usually go back to Anna's house. We have lunch and hang out for the afternoon.

"What did you think of youth group today?" asked Anna.

"I really enjoyed it. Mark is great. I'm quite excited

about the Jesus challenge. What did you think?" I replied.

"I'm not sure. I think it could be really difficult to keep thinking about Jesus while we're at school and stuff."

"I'm sure it will be fine." I was starting to get quite excited about our new challenge. Anna is the more confident of the two of us, but I think I'm the one that's more up for a challenge. I think Mark's a great youth pastor, so when he suggests stuff like this to us I feel myself rising to the challenge. Anna on the other hand, seems to be less excited about Mark's challenges. I'm not really sure why.

For the rest of the walk to Anna's I was caught up in a daydream about all these new challenges in my life. Dreaming about my part in the school play and now with this new challenge I'd become a much better Christian. My faith was about to take a huge leap forward with imagining Jesus as one of my friends. And I was really starting to get noticed at school now that I was an actress. I was excited. Life was on the brink of opening up to a whole new episode, my life would be completely transformed. Or so I thought.

Chapter 6 - Andrew

All too soon it was Monday morning and double Maths.

David was in his usual sarcastic mood.

"Hey Anderson, have you learned your lines yet, or do you need some help with that too?"

I stared back at him, hopefully with an annoyed look on my face.

"Or have you just spent the whole weekend hanging out with your little group of friends?"

At his mention of friends I realised that I had forgotten all about the challenge of being with teenage Jesus. Maybe this wasn't going to be as easy as I thought. But if David was typical of a fourteen year old boy, how could the prospect of hanging out with teenage Jesus be appealing? Although, I guess Jesus would be a lot nicer than David.

I started thinking about the other boys in class, desperately hoping for some inspiration. Trying to find a boy who I could model teenage Jesus on. I looked around Maths class to see if any of the boys would provide me with some inspiration.

There are the sporty guys, like Jim and Ben, who are

both in junior football leagues and are desperately hoping to play in the premier league when they leave school. There are the "cool" guys, like Kenneth and David, who spend their weekends at the shops and hang out with their "cool" friends. There are geek type guys, like Adam and Graham, who spend their time between homework and computer games. Then there are the tough guys; thankfully I don't have any of those guys in Maths class.

None of these guys were really fitting what I was hoping for. I just don't hang out with guys that much, so I wasn't really sure how to go about this task. With a bit of surprise I realised that the guy I speak to most is David, but obviously he's not a good example, as all we do is argue.

Later on, as Anna and I were queueing up for lunch, I noticed David just a bit further behind us in the queue. He was talking to Andrew. Suddenly I was inspired. Of course, Andrew. Can't believe I didn't make the connection yesterday. I'm not trying to raise him to a status he shouldn't have, but he is a Christian guy and he is fourteen, so he can be my inspiration for imagining teenage Jesus is with me now.

But what does Andrew do? I'm not really sure, I've never paid that much attention to him before.

"Hey Anna, why don't we use Andrew as our inspiration for our *What If* challenge?"

She burst out laughing at my suggestion. But then on seeing that I was serious she managed to stop her giggles.

"Think about it," I continued, "neither of us hangs out with guys, so watching Andrew might give us some real insight."

"Rachel, I don't think we really need to get bogged down in how fourteen year old guys act. I think it's more about thinking about Jesus with us, and how that could change our lives."

I decided not to pursue the point further with Anna. But I was right, I knew I was. This was a great way to get my thoughts tuned into the task at hand. It would be too easy to let Mark's challenge float on by without really thinking about it. Observing Andrew would help get my head around the task. I felt really pleased with myself for coming up with this idea.

I looked back down the dinner queue to see what Andrew was doing now. But as I looked back at Andrew, David looked over at me. I felt a rush of red spread through my face. Oh my stupid blushes, now David's going to think I was looking at him and that I was looking at him because I fancy him. I need to be more careful. I turned back to Anna and started chatting to her about the lunch options, desperate for something to distract me from looking back over at David and Andrew.

The afternoon passed by smoothly, and then it was time for my favourite part of the week, rehearsals. I was loving being in the school play. I loved rehearsing. I loved being part of it all. I loved meeting new people, my fellow actors. I even loved learning my lines. And, I loved the thrill of being on stage.

Rehearsal was going well, everyone seemed to be on good form. At three points in the play the actors get a mini-break while the first and second year pupils sing. Mr Smith and Mr Young had decided that the choir and the band would be over to the left of the stage. Mr Smith had also decided that to accommodate the choir in as small a space as possible that he would have them arranged on two benches. That way the back row could stand on their benches as they sang so they could be seen. Mr Young had the band seated to the side of the choir.

It was during the second choir performance that

chaos happened. A second year boy, called Alan, was at the end of the bench, nearest the band. The song they were singing was quite a lively one, and the choir had to sway from side to side and clap their hands. Everyone was getting into it so much that they weren't paying enough attention to where their feet were. Alan was getting more and more animated as the song went on until suddenly he toppled off of the bench.

Unfortunately, or fortunately depending on how you look at it, he fell right onto Fiona! Fiona, being a violin player, was sitting, somehow Alan managed to avoid her violin and fell into her lap. Fiona screamed and jumped up, which in turn knocked her seat into David, who was behind Fiona. David also plays the violin. Only he wasn't as lucky as Fiona. His bow got knocked back and scraped against his cheek. It caught him at a bad angle and cut his face.

What a scene was before us all. Alan was lying on the floor, rolling around in pain, clutching his ankle. Fiona was in a major strop and demanding an apology from the injured Alan. And David was just sitting on his chair in shock at the sight of blood pouring from his face. I did actually feel sorry for him, he just looked so confused and dazed.

Fiona seemed oblivious to the fact that her boyfriend was hurt and stunned. I wondered why Mrs Walsh had decided to give the part of Jemma to me rather than Fiona. Fiona has just proven what a complete drama queen she is!

Despite feeling sorry for David, I also felt a bit of delight in watching him. He always makes out that he's so cool and resourceful, and yet here he is stunned by the smallest of scratches. But I felt a slight reproach as I watched Andrew turn to talk to his friend, to make sure he was okay. Watching Andrew reminded me about Jesus being with me. I'm sure Jesus wouldn't be laughing at people for being injured, he would act like Andrew and make sure they were okay. I guess this just proves my point that it's a good idea to keep an eye on Andrew and think about Jesus.

In amongst all the commotion Miss Green was the first to realise that this effectively meant rehearsals were over. "Okay, everyone, that's it for today. Please make your way out of the hall now. We'll see you all back here on Thursday."

As I was packing up my bag to leave, Claire came over to me.

"Hey Rachel, how you getting on?"

"Great." I replied.

"Listen, I'm throwing a wee party for the drama group at my house next Friday. Do you think you would be able to make it?"

Oh my goodness, now I'm being invited to a party at Claire's house! Does life get any better than this?

"That would be great, yeah, I can make it." I heard myself reply. Why did I say that? There is no way my mum and dad would let me go to a party. Especially when it involves older teens. They would freak out about this. They would never let me go. And yet, *What If?*

Chapter 7 - Biology

I felt as if I floated to school the next day. I was still on a high from Claire asking me to her party, and on top of all that Tuesdays are my favourite day. On Tuesdays I have double periods of both Geography and Biology, my best subjects. The only negative on this particular Tuesday was trying to work out how I was going to be able to go to the party. But there had to be a way to make it work out.

Being a bit more enthusiastic on Tuesdays, I was at school before Anna and Julie. Our seats in registration class are next to the windows. It's a great place to sit as it means that on the mornings I go to school on my own, I can just sit and stare out of the window until either Anna or Julie arrives.

As I looked out of the window I watched lots of the other pupils walking into the school building. Some were walking quite enthusiastically, others were dragging their heels. Body language does tell people so much about your mood and attitude to something. As well as the other kids, I could also watch the teachers arriving at school and going into the staff entrance.

Most of my teachers are pretty decent, but there's always the exception to the rule. And here comes one of them now! Mr Gibb, my Biology teacher. Despite his best efforts, I really do enjoy Biology. He's not a very good teacher. He picks on me a lot. Thankfully he's not scary, so it doesn't really bother me that much when he moans at me. He just kind of seems a bit pathetic, actually. Sometimes I wonder why he became a teacher, the job seems to give him no satisfaction. Because I like Biology so much, I don't mind looking stuff up on the internet, learning more about the various things we're studying. It does make me appreciate that I get Mr Thomson for Maths, because if I got a teacher like Mr Gibb for Maths I'd have no hope at all.

My thoughts were interrupted by Anna and Julie coming into the class. By the time we'd had our morning catch up chat the bell rang for the start of first period.

First up double Biology. Biology is always a fun class. Firstly, like I said, because I like the subject. Secondly because Julie is in Biology with me and there is always something to have a good laugh about. And, as this is the only class that Andrew is in with me, it will give me a chance to observe him, see what kind of student he is.

Today we're doing some study on worms and woodlice. Whenever we study mini beasts Mr Gibb always asks someone to collect some from their garden or park to bring to class. For once he hadn't asked me to bring them in. However, the kids who were supposed to be supplying today's specimens forgot to bring them. But for some bizarre reason Mr Gibb decided that I was the one who should go out round the school grounds and bring back some worms. Honestly! Why am I the one punished for other people's forgetfulness? I think Mr Gibb thinks I enjoy his class too much and need to be punished like this whenever possible.

"Sir, why don't you make Brian or Kate go out to get the worms?" I said. "They're the ones who forgot them in the first place." I knew there was no point in arguing the case with him, but I decided to try, just in case he was in a good mood.

"Rachel go out and get those worms. I'm not asking Brian or Kate, I'm telling you," replied Mr Gibb in his usual gruff manner. One thing is for sure, he does his best to put me off Biology.

"Can I take Julie out with me to help?" A reasonable request I would say.

"No, Julie will stay here and take notes for you. Out you go now or we won't have time to study the worms."

So off I went to try and find worms. Our school playground is surrounded by bushes and grass, so there are lots of places that are good for finding worms! I was armed with a bucket of soapy water, a tried and tested way of bringing worms to the surface. I picked an area of grass next to a fallen tree trunk and poured out some of the soapy water. Oh gross, here come some wiggly heads up to the surface. This is the bit I hate, having to pick them up. Yuk!

I was so engrossed in trying to pick up the worms I didn't hear the footsteps approaching.

"Do you need some help here?"

I screamed out of surprise and fright. I lost my balance and landed on my bum, and I lost my grip on the worm I was busy pulling out of the ground. I looked round to see Andrew standing behind me.

"Andrew. You gave me the fright of my life," I said.

He just laughed and bent down beside me to help pull out some of the worms that were rising to the surface.

Here was a chance to get to talk to Andrew, to find out more about him. But I didn't have a clue what to say to him. We worked together in silence for a little while as we both pulled out some worms.

"So are you enjoying performing for the school play?" I asked him.

"Yeah, it's okay. I'd much rather play the guitar or drums instead of the violin, but it's what I'm doing just now. What about you, are you enjoying your acting?"

"I'm loving it. It's so much fun."

"How many of these worms do you think we need for class?" he asked.

"I think we've got enough now. Time to go back to class to the friendly Mr Gibb."

"I've noticed he seems to like giving you extra tasks."

"I know, I don't know what I've done to annoy him."

"Or maybe he thinks you're someone he can trust."

Never thought of that before, but I doubt it.

"Ah, Rachel, finally. How many worms have you got for us?" asked Mr Gibb. Funny how some teachers seem to find it quite acceptable to be rude to pupils, while other teachers treat us so much more like grown ups. I really don't think Andrew is right, if Mr Gibb thought I was someone he could trust surely he would be nicer to me, rather than barking out commands at me.

"We've got six, sir. One for each group."

"Okay then, hand them out round the groups. Right class lets get started. Look at your worksheets and start with exercise one on page six. I want each group to study their worm and complete the lesson through to exercise five at the end of the next page. Any questions? No. On you go then," ordered Mr Gibb.

"I don't believe him," I whispered to Julie, "I don't understand why he always picks on me."

"I know. It's so unfair. And he's so obvious about it."

As Julie and I sat and worked through the worm exercises I wondered how Jesus views worms. After all he was there when God was making everything from the lovely animals to the yucky beasties. But if there's one thing you do learn in Biology it's that everything has its process and purpose in the eco-system. Even these little worms have their place.

Julie and I worked in relative silence, trying not to do anything that would draw Mr Gibb's attention to us any further. As we were working it occurred to me that Julie might be my best chance of getting to Claire's party. She lives near Claire, so maybe I could ask Julie if I could go to her's next Friday night, and then from there go to Claire's. It wasn't the best scenario, and not a great deal for Julie, but hopefully she'd be okay with it. And I did so want to go to Claire's party.

Later on as I walked over to the canteen with Julie I told her all about Claire inviting me to her party. And how I'd love to be able to go but that my parents would never let me.

"Why don't you tell your parents you're coming over to mine after school on Friday?" suggested Julie.

Brilliant!. This was just what I was hoping she would say.

"You can have dinner at mine then head over to Claire's. She lives in the street next to mine. Then you can tell your dad to pick you up from my place at ten o'clock. And they'll never have to know."

Julie's parents let her have a lot more freedom than mine, so she was quite happy to let me use her as an excuse for some freedom of my own. I was so excited that she'd taken the hint, without me having to push too much. I realised it wasn't a fair use of friendship but I was going to Claire's party. Yeah!

Just as we agreed the arrangements for Friday, Anna joined us. "What you talking about?" she asked. Before I could get a word in, Julie updated her on my party invitation and the arrangements we were making. Anna didn't have to say anything, I could tell she didn't like it.

"Why don't you just ask your parents if you can go?" suggested Anna.

"Oh come on Anna, you know what my parents are like; they're not as cool as your parents. There is no way they would let me go to a party, especially when it's older kids that are having it and Claire's parents won't be there."

"You don't know that for sure, why don't you just ask them and see."

"Because if they say I can't go, then I won't be able to go round to Julie's either, and I won't get to the party. But this way they can't say no, I'll be allowed to go to Julie's and they'll never know."

"It'll be fine," said Julie, "it's a perfect plan. What could possible go wrong?"

I tried to push away my feelings of doubt and uncertainty about the plan. I hadn't wanted Anna to find out so quickly. I knew she would pull me up on my dishonesty.

As we had lunch, I persuaded myself it would all be fine. *What If* I could actually pull this off?

Chapter 8 – Wine Gums

Tuesday afternoons consist of English and Geography. I quite like English, but Geography is the best. I love finding out about the various geological features, like equatorial rain forests, caves, glaciers, etc. It's great finding out about these amazing aspects of creation: how they came about; how they work with the habitat. It all fascinates me. When I'm older I'd love to travel to countries where I could see some of these things for myself and not just read about it in textbooks and on the internet.

Anna sits next to me in Geography. Funny how the classes you're in with friends always seem that bit better. Good company is definitely a positive thing. Unfortunately David and Fiona are also in my Geography class, but at least they sit over at the other side of the class. And unlike with Maths, I actually understand Geography and get good grades in it, so I'm not such an obvious target for David here.

The other good thing about Geography is having a great teacher. Mr Niel is the best teacher in the department. He's fun and makes the classes interesting. He obviously experienced life in the 1970s. He's still got the beard to prove it. And a slight look of the 70s in his clothing choices. But despite the look he is bang up to date with what high school pupils are going through and has a real rapport with all of his classes.

At the moment we are studying rivers, how they form and why they follow the course they do. It's not the most exciting of topics but offers the big advantage of a field trip in a couple of weeks. Through the course of the year we'll make four trips to the river to see how it changes from autumn to winter to spring to summer. Four field trips from one topic. Brilliant! These are the things I love about Geography - it's a practical subject. It gives meaning to the world around. And it gets you out of classes every so often.

After about twenty minutes of class there was a knock on the classroom door. Miss McDonald asked Mr Niel if she could speak with him outside. Miss McDonald seems ancient. I think she's taught at the school forever. But despite the fact she's been a teacher for so long, she seems to have no idea how to teach, or how to control a class. Mr Niel is the head of department so she always comes to him for help when she has issues with her class. And that seems to happen quite frequently.

Mr Niel came back into the class after a few minutes. "Start reading about the mature stage of the river from your textbooks class. I'll be back in ten minutes." He looked quite annoyed. I think he hates having to deal with Miss McDonald's classes. We heard Miss McDonald's classroom door slam shut and Mr Niel shouting at her class. Mr Niel is a great teacher, but can be really quite scary when he needs to be.

Anna and I opened up our books and started reading. With Mr Niel forced into one of his scary moods, we wanted to make sure we did as he asked. Others in the class had different ideas.

Fiona and David sit with a group of their friends. As soon as Mr Niel had slammed the door in the other classroom they all turned round and started talking to each other. I think they were making their conversation loud on purpose for all to hear. They were talking about a party John, one of their crew, had at his house on Saturday night. It was obvious they all thought they were all cool and grown up. They wanted the whole class to hear about their exploits. They were all laughing about one of the guys who had got drunk. Making it sound as if he couldn't handle his drink, but they could.

"Did you see Gary?" asked David. "It was hilarious. The guy could hardly stand up, never mind dance. After just a couple of bottles of beer he was wasted."

"Yeah," laughed one of his friends. "He got Sally up to dance and then fell over her foot. I think he can forget going out with her any time soon."

They all laughed.

I made the mistake of looking over. Fiona saw me.

"What about Rachel, guys," she laughed. "Bet she'd get drunk just eating a packet of Wine Gums." They all laughed. Fiona had a smug look on her face. Knowing she had managed to put me down in front of the whole class. But David didn't laugh, he just looked over at me with a strange expression.

Why do people do that? Why do they take such pleasure in making other people look bad? How do they manage to make you out to be such a goody goody without you even saying anything? I felt like the most boring person in the class. It's not like I've never had a drink. Mum and dad let me have small glasses of wine with special dinners. But I don't see what all the big fuss over wine is. The times I've tried it I've never really liked it that much.

I'm much happier just with a coke. But that definitely seems to put me in the boring camp.

But I'd show her. Just wait till she found out that I was going to be at Claire's party. I suddenly realised there was a chance that Fiona and David might be invited too. That would be a disaster. I felt my fighting spirit wear off pretty quickly with that thought.

Anna put her hand on my arm. She gave me a look of reassurance. I could feel my face burning red as the group continued to laugh at my expense.

"Are you sure you want to be at a party with them?" asked Anna, also realising there was a good chance they'd be at Claire's. "Think about how they treat you, do you really want to hang out with them out of school?"

Between Anna's comments that I should talk to mum and dad about the party, and the realisation that Fiona and David would be at the party, it wasn't looking such a fun night after all.

Chapter 9 – More Lines

On Thursday morning my registration teacher handed me a note. It was from Mrs Walsh; she wanted to see me at morning break. I wondered why she wanted to see me?

For the first two classes my mind was working overtime as to why Mrs Walsh would want to see me. All my thoughts were negative, of course. Worrying that she was pulling my part from the play. That she'd decided I was no good as Jemma, and was going to recast it or give the part to someone else. What If she gave the part to Fiona? It would be a disaster if that happened. Fiona would never let me live it down, she would go on and on about it forever. With every negative thought I could feel the panic spread further through my body.

At the appropriate time I headed over to the drama department.

"Tell me Rachel," said Mrs Walsh, "are you enjoying being in the school play?"

"Yes, I'm loving it," I said, still unsure of where the conversation was leading.

"That's good, because I'm very pleased with your

acting ability and the dedication you're showing to the play." I felt myself relax, at least a little bit, it didn't sound like she was about to throw me out of the play.

"I've been speaking to Miss Green and to Claire and we've decided that we would like to increase the part of Jemma."

Wow! I was speechless.

"I realise time is marching on, and the show is next Friday, so we're just making a small change. Jemma will now give all of the closing speech. So instead of the current arrangement, where you give part of the closing speech with Gareth and Samantha, you will now be doing the whole thing yourself. Will you be able to learn those lines okay for next   Monday?"

"Yes," was all the reply I could manage.

"Good, then we'll practise it this afternoon, you can use your script today, then you'll need to do it by heart at Monday's rehearsal."

As I walked into rehearsal that afternoon I felt like I was floating on air, and not for the first time since I had been involved in the show. Anna and Julie were really excited about the extension of my part. Even if it was only a few more lines, mine was the last voice the audience would hear from the show. It was really quite exciting.

To add to the excitement Claire came over to me and gave me a great big hug. "I'm so excited for you, Rachel. It's great that Mrs Walsh has extended the part for you."

"And thank you for agreeing with her," I replied.

"Attention everyone," shouted Mrs Walsh. "There is a slight change to the ending of the play. Instead of having the last part read by Rachel, Gareth and Samantha, it will now just be read by Rachel."

As I looked around I could see that Gareth and

Samantha didn't look overly happy at having their parts reduced, but I couldn't blame them for that. Claire looked over at me with a big encouraging smile. Fiona looked shocked, as if a huge big injustice had just been committed. And David looked as if he was smirking. Why would he be smirking?

The rehearsal went well. It was fun having the extra lines and getting to be the person who finished off the play. My part had gone from being one of the smallest parts to being one of some importance. I felt really excited, and, I must admit, a bit proud of myself.

I had read the script so many times I knew quite a lot of the play off by heart already. So when it came to my extra lines I only had to glance down at my script a couple of times as a reminder of what I was to say.

As we were leaving the hall Fiona pushed past me. "Well excuse me," she said, "do you think you're so important now that you don't even need to let people past."

"But I was standing still, you were the one walking, there was plenty of room for you to get past without bumping into me."

She gave a haughty kind of noise, thrust her nose up in the air, and walked off as if she was the injured party.

David was walking behind her. He looked like he was taking pleasure in the whole thing. And then as he walked past he winked at me! Honestly, I'm loving being in the school play, but it doesn't half bring out some weird emotions and behaviour in people.

I can't believe David winked at me.

Chapter 10 – The Shopping Centre

I was glad it was Saturday; school seemed to be getting a bit too intense. Julie, Anna and myself were out for a day of shopping, then I was going to stay over at Anna's, followed by church on Sunday. Thinking of church made me realise I had yet again forgotten about teenage Jesus. I guess I'm not so good at involving Jesus in every aspect of my life. I put it down to not seeing enough of Andrew at school to remind me of the challenge. But then the whole Andrew thing took a new twist.

We were in our favourite shop, browsing along the clothes rails, when all of a sudden I spotted Andrew. What was he doing here? He was walking through the girls' section, to get to the back of the store to where the guys' stuff was. At first I thought he was on his own, but then to my horror I spotted David, and realised the two of them were out shopping together.

I casually looked through the rail of clothes in front of me and picked out a top, all the while I was watching Andrew to see what he was doing. The two of them were wandering about having a look through the jeans and t-shirts. It looked like it was David who was the one searching for something new, no surprise there I guess. After about ten minutes they must have decided there was nothing of interest for David and started walking back towards where I was standing. I quickly turned my back. It worked, they hadn't seen me. But then curiosity got the better of me and I wanted to see where they were heading next. After all Andrew was my example of what fourteen year old boys do, so I had to observe a bit more of this out of school action. I just had to make sure they didn't see me.

Slowly and quietly I followed them to the front of the shop to see where they would go next. They walked out of the shop and turned left, I walked up to the entrance of the shop to get a better view of where they were going. I didn't want to leave the shop because Julie and Anna were still there, and I didn't want to get too close to the guys anyway, I just wanted to see where they would go next.

As they walked further away it was difficult for me to see where they were headed. Were they going to another shop? Were they going for something to eat? Or were they giving up and leaving the shops? I edged my way further forward, desperately trying to catch a glimpse of what they were going to do.

All of a sudden the shop alarm went off. Within a second the horror of the situation had sunk in. I had forgotten that I was still carrying the top, and had got too close to the door security alarm and set it off. A large, scary looking security man came towards me. But worst of all Andrew and David looked round and saw me, and saw the security man grab hold of my arm. I'm not sure if my face was white with shock or red with embarrassment. Ground please swallow me now!

I caught sight of David doubled over laughing, and Andrew looking confused before the security man turned me around back into the shop.

"Honestly, I promise I wasn't trying to steal it," I pleaded to the security man and the shop assistant. "I'd just seen someone I recognised and went to the door to see where they were going." Which wasn't a lie. At this point Julie and Anna came running over, having realised it was me at the centre of the commotion. As Julie worked out what was going on, she said, "Obviously she wasn't trying to steal the top, why would she just be standing at the door with it if she was trying to do a runner with it." Her reasoning seemed to make sense to the security guard and the sales assistant and I was let off with a warning.

Julie and Anna knew I would be mortified by the whole thing. "Time for lunch," said Anna, as a way to try and distract me.

But things didn't improve. We ended up at the Burger Bar. But of course who had to be there already? Andrew and David. I didn't notice them until we were sitting down. I could feel my face flush red just seeing them. I could barely eat any lunch for thinking about what had just happened. I guess this answered the question of where the guys were heading after I saw them in the shop.

"What's wrong with you?" asked Anna.

I nodded over to where David and Andrew were sitting. Anna followed my nod and saw the guys.

"Please tell me it wasn't something to do with them that you set off the security alarm in the shop?"

My sheepish smile gave her the answer she needed.

As I looked up I could see David and Andrew walking over to our table. Could this get any more embarrassing?

"So Anderson," said David, "what is it? Can you not keep away from me? Are you just pulled to my magnetic personality?"

"Oh for goodness sake David! Get over yourself. I

wasn't even looking at you, I was watching Andrew."

You could have heard a pin drop. Julie and Anna both swung round to look at me, their jaws wide open. Andrew looked mortified, and then suddenly David burst out laughing. I'm sure if he'd stopped to think about it he'd have had a hurt ego, but as it was, he was able to see yet another reason to make fun of me. I really must learn to think more before I speak!

I could still hear his laughter as he walked away. Julie and Anna were staring at me, not sure what to say. So Julie just changed the conversation to talking about clothes shopping again.

After some more shopping we said goodbye to Julie as she went home. Then Anna and I caught the bus back to Anna's house.

"Okay, Rachel, now that it's just us, tell me everything about what happened today."

I told her all about me watching Andrew, and how that had led to the security alarm going off.

"Rachel I told you that watching Andrew wasn't really the point of the whole *What If* teenager Jesus was here. Mark was just giving us that as a starting point for our thoughts.

"Do you want to know who I've been thinking about for this challenge?"

"Who?" I replied quietly.

"You!"

"Me!" I said, no longer in my quiet voice. "Why on earth would you think about me?"

"Because we're supposed to be thinking that if Jesus was here in person now, he'd be hanging out with us. And who do I hang out with most? You."

There was no denying that, but still, why would thinking about me help her think about Jesus. As if reading my mind she continued.

"I've been thinking about how we spend our time together and about what Jesus would be doing with us during that time. Would he be watching TV with us? Listening to music with us? Helping us work out school issues."

"Yeah, maybe I have been making this all too complicated."

Anna laughed. "Oh Rachel, you always make everything too complicated."

We both laughed. Anna really is my best friend.

"I guess you were right, Anna. I am struggling to think about Jesus as being one of our friends. I am struggling to have all the different bits of my life fit together, and to remember Jesus in all the different situations I'm in."

"Yeah, I know," said Anna, "it's hard for me too. Tell you what, why don't we chat about it each evening. Tell each other about our days, and where Jesus was with us."

"That's a great idea."

"And of course, regarding Andrew, you know you're going to have to explain all this to him tomorrow at church," said Anna.

"No, I'm sure he won't want to be anywhere near me tomorrow, never mind have me speak to him."

"Rachel, you need to speak to him and straighten it all out. Otherwise he's going to have the wrong idea of what happened."

Yet again I realised Anna was right. But it didn't stop me wishing that Andrew wouldn't be at church tomorrow and that I wouldn't need to have yet another embarrassing conversation.

Chapter 11 - Consequences

I stayed the night at Anna's and then we went to church together in the morning.

As I sat next to Anna I was painfully aware of the task that lay before me. Andrew was sitting two rows in front of us, so I had a constant reminder the whole way through church that I had to speak to him and apologise.

At the end of church I went over to Andrew. "Hey Andrew, I'm really sorry about yesterday, and in fact for all of last week."

"Yeah, maybe we need to talk," he replied. "Let's grab a cola."

We went up to the youth church area and got a drink. I felt really awkward and unsure of how to explain myself. Would he think I was crazy? Would he even believe me? But we ended up having a really great chat. I had no idea he was such a nice guy. I told him all about my struggle to try and picture Jesus as a teenager now, and how I'd been using him as a reminder model. I thought his face was going to explode with embarrassment at that point. "Rachel, you're crazy. Why would you use me as the model when you've got such good friends of your own?" Funny, I seem to remember Anna saying something very similar. But I maintain my idea was a good one, apart from a few flaws!

We then got onto talking about the play. Which then led to talking about my issues with Fiona and David. But then Andrew surprised me by saying, "Try going a bit easier on David. He doesn't actually have life as easy as he makes out. There's a lot of tough stuff going on behind the scenes there. What you see isn't always the real him."

"Oh, come on. There's no way David has it tough."

"No I'm serious. And off the record he does actually like you. He thinks you're fun, and different from the other girls at school, they're all girly and trying to be older than their years. You're the only girl who speaks back to him, the others see him as either a no-go area or are desperately waiting for him to ask them out."

"Really?" I was speechless. I didn't know what to say. Could this be a true picture of David? Or was Andrew actually being mean to me, and just winding my up? No, Andrew wouldn't do that.

"I'm not kidding you on Rachel. Just don't tell David I said any of this stuff to you. I just thought it was time you knew that there's stuff going on in the background that makes life complicated for him."

I really didn't know what to think about Andrew's revelations. I was confused. *What If* this was all true, and David wasn't the person I thought he was?

But any kind thoughts I might have been starting to have towards David vanished as I walked into Maths class on Monday morning. As soon as I was at my desk David was laughing at me about Saturday.

"Hey Anderson, do you want me to set you up with my mate Andrew?" he laughed. "I must say I'm not used to setting up my friends, usually the girls want *me*!"

I stared at him in disbelief. No, there was no way Andrew could have been right about the behind the scenes David. He was full of himself through and through and surely that could only be the case with someone who had life good and easy.

But the consequences from Saturday didn't stop there. Even on Wednesday I was still paying the price. Fiona scowled at me as I sat beside her in Home Ec, nothing new in that.

"Rachel I hope you don't have any thoughts on making a move on Andrew," she said.

"What?"

"I heard about you following him at the shops on Saturday. He's out of reach for you. Mandy likes him, and is planning on going to the Christmas party with him. So forget about him, he's spoken for."

What is wrong with the world? How come what I do gets taken totally out of context. If I was interested in Andrew it wouldn't be anyone else's business, but somehow I'm in the wrong, again. But it's okay for those in the "group" to fancy him. Again Fiona had succeeded in making me feel boring and excluded from her world.

That night I went over to Anna's. We had decided it would be a good idea to come up with some stuff on what teenage Jesus would be like. To get us started we did an internet search on Jesus as a teenager, but that just brought up some weird references. So we decided we were going to have to be creative ourselves.

We started off by describing his physical appearance, and then went on to talk about his character traits, then thought about what activities he might be into. We even drew pictures of what we thought he would look like. We spent an hour putting together a picture and description of what we thought Jesus would be like as a teenager. Anna is more creative than me, and definitely a better artist. We decided that two heads were better than one when it came to creative thinking. But even though I'd gotten things a bit wrong with watching Andrew, I still thought of that as an easier way for me to think about the Jesus challenge.

Once we'd finished our picture I told Anna all about my run ins with David and Fiona regarding the whole thing with Andrew.

"Rachel, you got yourself into a scrape and now you just need to weather the storm. They will forget about it soon enough. You know what the two of them are like. They love nothing more than winding you up."

I wasn't sure if I should tell Anna about what Andrew had told me about David. Would that be gossiping? But I decided that if Jesus was here I'd be telling him about it and asking his advice, so I decided to tell Anna.

Anna seemed as surprised as I was with this new discovery. But I told her that with David's comments to me on Monday I had quickly lost any sympathy I had felt towards him.

"I think you just need to keep this in the background. Obviously, don't say anything to him about it. But just remember when he's giving you a hard time that things might be tough for him."

Relationships are hard. This is all feeling very complicated.

Chapter 12 – The Party

Finally, after all the ups and downs of the week we reached Friday, the day of the party. I was so excited, but I did feel a bit guilty at having lied to my parents about it.

At the end of school I met Julie at the school gates and went back to her place. While I was there I didn't even see her parents. I was glad about that. I didn't want to have to include any more people in my lie than I absolutely had too. Julie really didn't mind at all about me using her as an excuse, she seemed glad to help get me to the party. Maybe she felt sorry for me because my parents are more strict than hers. She even helped me put some make up on before I left, which I was very grateful for as I'm not very good at the make up side of things. I was wearing my favourite jeans and the new top I'd bought, after the embarrassing incident, at the shopping centre on Saturday.

"You look fab," said Julie.

"Thanks. And thanks for covering for me and letting me get to the party."

"You are welcome Cinderella, now just be back here by ten, and you'll be fine, your folks will never know."

I felt a twinge of guilt as she said that. But then with a final check in the mirror, and yet another thank you to Julie, I headed out of her house and round to Claire's.

As I walked along the street my doubts started getting the better of me. Did I really want to be putting myself in a party setting with Fiona and David? Wasn't it just setting myself up for a bad experience? And my guilt at lying to mum and dad was getting stronger. It was one thing to be all talk, it was another thing to actually go through with it. This was the first time I'd done anything like this, maybe that was why I was feeling so guilty. Was this really such a big deal? Was this just another thing that I was making too complicated? But after our *What If* challenge at church I was feeling guilty about that too. I'm sure if Jesus was part of my group of friends he would be telling me I shouldn't be lying to my parents, just like Anna had said.

It seemed as if there were more reasons to turn around and walk away from the party than there were to go. As I continued walking towards Claire's house, my pace slowed down, and I really did think that maybe I should just turn round and go back to Julie's, but then I met up with a group of the fourth year pupils. I got so caught up in chatting with them I didn't even realise that we had reached Claire's house.

As I walked into her house Claire came over to welcome me. She is so friendly, I like her a lot. I looked around the room to see who else was there. Thankfully there was no sign of Fiona or David yet.

I walked into the dining room with the fourth year pupils I had came in with. Claire had a good play list set up on her mp3 player and everyone seemed in good mood, ready to enjoy a fun party. Claire had set out some plates with crisps and chocolates, and a table with drinks. She had soft drinks, but also beer and a bottle of vodka. I helped myself to a can of cola and crisps. After half an hour there was still no sign of Fiona or David, I felt myself relax and began to enjoy the party.

I was standing talking to one of the fourth year girls when we became aware of a disturbance in the living room. A group of us walked through to see what was going on.

"Come on, dance with me!" said a rather drunk sounding Gary, Fiona and David's friend. I guess they were right about Gary, he really didn't seem to be able to hold his drink. He'd obviously had too much to drink again. And as they had described from his previous party experience, he was once again trying to get some girl to dance with him. But due to his level of intoxication she was having none of it.

His face turned very pale, he looked a bit worried and then ran to the toilet, we could all hear the sounds of retching as he started being sick.

Wow, this guy really wasn't learning from his past experiences. Claire's friend Sophie rushed after Gary, grabbing some towels and cloths from the kitchen on the way. I don't think it was so much concern for Gary, as concern for Claire and helping her keep the house in order.

"He does this at every party," said Claire as she came over to stand beside me. "He was at a party just last week and did exactly the same thing."

So I guess Fiona and David move in the same social scene as Claire, wonder why they're not here?

As if reading my mind, Claire continued, "I'm surprised he's been allowed to come tonight. You're in classes with Fiona and David aren't you?"

"Yes," I replied, waiting to find out if she was going to start singing their praises.

"I'd invited them tonight too, but neither of them were allowed to come. Their parents weren't too happy hearing about what went on last weekend, so there are no parties for them for the next couple of weeks."

So after all of Fiona's comments to me in Geography class, turns out she's not the wild, party goer she makes out. Although, I realised the only reason I was at this party was because my parents didn't know I was here.

Having been empowered with this new information I started to enjoy the party. With the knowledge that Fiona and David wouldn't be here all my other doubts seemed to disappear too. My feelings of guilt were gone and I felt a new confidence to mingle with my fellow partiers. I even accepted a bottle of beer from one of the guys.

The party was in full swing, I was having a great time. I'd chatted to most people there, and had even been up dancing for a while. But then suddenly, as with Cinderella, I heard the clock chiming and realised with shock that it was already ten o'clock. I had to get back round to Julie's on the double. My dad was picking me up there at ten. I had to make sure I got into her garden without him seeing me, so that he would think I had just came out of her house. This could be tricky.

I said a quick farewell and thanks to Claire and headed out of her house. I was so preoccupied with trying to work out how to get into Julie's garden without being seen that I didn't even see him standing on the pavement, and I bumped right into him.

"Dad!"

My eyes quickly took in the scene, but my brain couldn't work it out. Why was my dad standing at the side of our car, parked in front of Claire's house? But one thing my brain was able to work out in a flash was that he looked really angry.

How could I get myself out of this situation? I couldn't. I was well and truly caught!

Dad didn't even say anything to me. He just opened up the passenger door and waited for me to get in the car. I felt so ashamed. I could feel my cheeks burn red hot. The drive home seemed to take forever. He kept up his no speaking policy the whole way home. I wasn't sure if he was waiting to get home, or if he would never speak to me again. But it turned out he was waiting till we got back home. And then it wasn't just him, it was mum too.

"Rachel Elizabeth Anderson, how could you? How could you be so deceitful? How could you possibly think this was a good idea? Did you not think of the safety aspect?" said mum.

"We thought you were at Julie's house until you sent us the text to say you needed picked up," continued dad.

"What? What text?"

"The text you sent from your friend's phone. You said your battery was flat, so you were using a friend's phone, and asked if I would come and get you."

"I never sent you a text." I realised this was a mistake even as the words left my mouth. To me this was the complete shock of the whole situation. More than being caught, the knowledge that someone had landed me in it by texting my dad. But who? Who would do that?

Mum and dad went on and on about my dishonesty, but I didn't take in a word they said. All I could think about was the text that my dad received. Was it Anna? I knew she wasn't happy about me going to the party. She knew I was lying to my mum and dad about it, and she didn't agree with me doing that. I had put her lack of support down to her being jealous of my being invited to a party at Claire's house. But would Anna, my best friend, really do such a thing as text my dad, pretending it was me. It would be easy enough for her to do it. Her dad had my dad's mobile number, so she would easily be able to get his number.

I realised mum and dad had stopped yelling and were just looking at me.

"Didn't you hear me, Rachel?" asked mum. "Go to bed now."

I was glad to get to my own room. So much to think about. I had enjoyed the party. But what a way for it to end. And what was the deal with Anna, telling on me like that. I couldn't believe she would betray me like that. *What If* Anna wasn't the friend I thought she was?

Chapter 13 – Another Monday

The weekend had been a slow, tedious affair. I was grounded for the weekend, but I was okay with that. My bigger fear had been that I wouldn't be allowed to stay in the school play. Mum and dad had threatened to pull me out, but decided against it as it would affect other people too much.

Church on Sunday had done nothing to lift my mood. I had to stay with mum and dad rather than sit with Anna, but I was also okay with that, as there was still the question of whether or not she had been the one who had sent the text to dad.

My Monday morning gloom was stronger than ever as I left the house for school. I met Anna at her gate. We walked in silence for the first ten minutes, which wasn't that unusual on a Monday morning as it takes me so long to wake up, but we could both feel a tension that suggested silence was the best option.

But Anna is not one for letting tension have a place. "What's wrong?"

"Why did you send my dad a text to let him know I was at Claire's party?" I hadn't meant to accuse her so directly, but she had caught me off guard, so I just came right out with what I was thinking.

"I never sent your dad a text," she replied. "I wouldn't do that to you, Rachel. I don't think you should have gone to the party without telling your parents, but you're a big girl now, it's up to you to tell your parents. I'm not going to tell on you like some little kid. I can't believe you would even think I could do something like that to you."

"But then if you didn't text my dad, who did?" I replied, as if asking the question made me seem not quite so stupid, just that I'd accused the wrong person.

I had just accused Anna of not being a good friend. And yet she now showed what a good friend she really was by not falling out with me because of my stupidity. She seemed okay about letting it go, to forgive and forget. I don't think I would be so good.

"So how you getting on hanging out with Jesus?" she asked.

"Not so well. I don't think I would have seen much of him this weekend. For starters I was grounded, but even if I hadn't been, would he have wanted to be with me?"

"Why do you think he wouldn't?"

"Well if my mum and dad are mad at me for lying to them, how could I possibly think that Jesus would want to spend time with me?"

"Rachel! Jesus isn't going to stop being your friend because you lied to your parents and went to a party. Just like I'm not going to stop being your friend because of it. You did something wrong, and now you're feeling the guilt and the consequences. You made the wrong decision, we all do that."

I looked at Anna. Something was definitely different about her. She used to be the one that was less sure of her faith, but now she seems to be the stronger one. Maybe this *What If* challenge has really helped make Jesus real for her.

As usual talking to Anna made me feel better, especially seeing this new side to her. But as I got to school the negative doubts were there again, and by the time I walked into Maths I was feeling down. The weekend had been terrible, so I really didn't feel equipped to be dealing with Maths, let alone David. But the strangest thing happened. He was actually nice to me.

"Heard you were at Claire's party on Friday night," he said. "Did you have a good time?"

"Since when were you worried if I was enjoying myself?" I replied. But then I felt a bit guilty. After all, he had been nice to me for a change. But with David you just never knew if he actually was being nice, or you were just missing some sarcasm in his comment.

I thought again of the changes in Anna since she had been following Mark's Jesus challenge. Maybe I needed to get back on track with that. What would it be like if Jesus was in Maths class with me. Scary thing is, maybe he would be friends with David. And worst still, maybe he would expect me to be friends with David. Yikes! I decided that maybe I should try and be nicer to David, especially when, at least on the surface, he seemed to be in a friendly mood today. Plus there was the conversation I'd had with Andrew when he'd told me David had some issues. And on top of all that I felt guilty at the whole party incident, so I decided I needed to be on my best behaviour now.

Later on it was time for P.E., and another exciting encounter with hockey. As we left the nice warm changing rooms and went out to the cold hockey pitch, Fiona pushed past me.

"Hey Anderson, did your dad find you okay on Friday night?" And with that she went giggling off with a couple of her friends. I was left standing still, speechless. If I'd been one of those toon characters my eyes would have been bulging out and my chin would be hitting the ground.

Of course!

The incident from Friday night did have Fiona's signature stamp of meanness printed all over it. I couldn't believe I had ever thought of Anna as the guilty party when it had been Fiona. And then I remembered back to last week in our Home Ec class. Last week Fiona had asked to have a look at my mobile phone and said that she was thinking of getting one like mine. I had thought it odd at the time. After all, why would Fiona ever want to copy me when it came to mobile phones? But I had been so busy keeping an eye on the custard and making sure it didn't get any lumps in it, I had merely handed it over to her, and not really thought about it that much. Obviously she had got my dad's number from my contacts list when she had my phone. And then telling my dad I had to use her phone because mine was out of battery power was really quite devious.

I couldn't believe it though. I couldn't understand why someone would stoop so low. Spoiling my fun, just because she was grounded.

Was that why David had been nice to me in Maths? Because he knew what Fiona had done? Was he trying to somehow cover for her by being nice to me, in some kind of good-cop bad-cop scenario? Did he think that by being nice to me he would lower my defences for Fiona to come in with the surprise blow later on in the day? What a pair!

"Anna, did you hear what Fiona just said to me?"

"No, I couldn't hear her."

"She told me she sent my dad that text on Friday night. What do you think of that?"

Anna gave me a look of sympathy. I knew it, I could always count on Anna to be on my side.

"That's really bitchy of her, Rachel, but you kind of set yourself up by not telling your mum and dad yourself."

What? That's not what I was expecting.

"Anna, how can you say that? I thought you were on my side."

"I am on your side, but that doesn't mean that I agree with all the things you do. If you had asked your mum and dad if you could go to the party, then Fiona wouldn't have been able to land you in it. So you kind of did it to yourself."

I hate it when Anna's right. And she seems to be right more often than me these days.

Chapter 14 - The Worst Day

On Wednesday things went downhill even more.

My third class on Wednesday mornings is Home Economics. I don't mind cooking and baking, but I hate doing it at school. I'm really slow moving around the kitchen, so I can never finish anything off in the time we have in class. Thankfully I only have to do one class of Home Ec in a week.

At our school if you achieve a reasonable level in your second year results you get to do Latin. But to fit it into your timetable you need to drop one class of Home Ec and one class of Music. At the end of last year, when I was given the option, I was happy to cut back on Home Ec and Music as I'm no good at either of these subjects. However, I am discovering, to my pain, that Latin is not a fun class to be in. Still it could be worse. Our class gets the "fun" teacher. The other group is taught by the headmaster, Mr Pierce. Thankfully I'm not in that class!

The other negative of Home Ec is that I need to sit next to Fiona. We're the only two in our Home Ec class who are in the Latin timetable so we need to work together, otherwise on the day we're not here someone else could be left without a partner.

Fiona really believes that she knows better than

everybody about everything. We always end up arguing about something: when the day's cooking project is ready; how much of an ingredient to put in; who can make the better cake, etc. Sometimes Fiona's right, sometimes I'm right. But we would never admit the other one is ever right.

Today's class is cooking fish and chips in the oven. I don't know why they think it's a good idea for us to cook any fish dishes, we'll all smell of fish for the rest of the day. Yuk!

The class started with all of us being given our portions of fish and chips. It should have been simple enough. All we had to do was put the fish and chips on a baking tray. Put it in the oven. Then take it back out in twenty minutes.

While the food was cooking in the oven our teacher, Mrs Clark, gave us one of those boring Home Ec chats about kitchen hygiene.

After fifteen minutes talking about the best method of cleaning cookers Mrs Clark told us we should check on the food and clear up our work areas. Fiona dashed to open the oven and pulled out the tray with the fish and chips. As usual, in her "I know best" voice, she announced, "Well obviously this is now ready, go and get the plates, Rachel." Without paying much attention to the food I walked over to take out a couple of plates from the cupboard and returned to where Fiona was standing at the open oven.

"The fish isn't ready yet, Fiona," I remarked.

"You don't know what you're talking about," she smugly replied.

"It needs to go back into the oven for another five minutes."

"Oh no it doesn't. Now hold the plates out and I'll serve out the fish."

Splat!

As Fiona tried to serve the fish I pulled the plates away. Just as stubborn as she was. We both stared at each other. Mrs Clark came running over to our work station.

"Rachel! Fiona! What on earth are you doing?"

"We were having a disagreement Miss about how cooked the fish was. I told Fiona to put it back in the oven, but she tried to put it on the plates as I was walking away," I attempted as an excuse.

"What a waste of school property. Clean this mess up at once. Then I want you to stay behind after class to talk about this further."

Fiona and I didn't even look at each other as we cleared everything up. As the end of class bell rang we both walked up to Mrs Clark's desk.

"Today you have both wasted school property, which is completely unacceptable behaviour. You will both complete a three hundred word essay for next class as to why this was wrong and why you should take more care with school property. I want these essays signed by your parents so that they know just what type of unruly behaviour you get up to in school." With that she told us to leave the room. Without even looking at each other, Fiona and I walked off in opposite directions.

A punishment exercise! This wasn't supposed to happen.

It was a relief to meet up with Anna and Julie for lunch.

"What's wrong with you?" asked Anna, seeing from my face that all was not well.

"I've just been given a punishment exercise from Mrs Clark," I replied.

I told the girls all about what happened in Home Ec. I couldn't believe it when both of them burst out laughing at the end of my story.

Just as I was finishing off my tale I saw Fiona walk past with her posh group of friends. I could tell from the looks being thrown in my direction that she had obviously been telling them all about Home Ec too.

"Come on," said Anna, "let's just get out of here and go and get some fresh air. Honestly Rachel, you take things too much to heart sometimes. You let things be bigger in your head than they actually are in reality. No one, not even Fiona, will remember this incident for long. Just put it down to bad luck."

I love when Anna knows exactly what to say to me. She's such a good friend. She knows just what to say to help me get over things in spite of myself. But I have this nagging feeling that Fiona certainly won't be forgetting about the ruined fish incident for quite some time, and that she'll be looking to cast it back at me at every opportunity.

As we got outside into the playground we spotted a large, noisy crowd gathering. This could only mean one thing - a fight. We rushed over to see what was going on. We could barely see over the kids in front of us, but we managed to catch glimpses of two boys hitting into each other. It's weird how playground fights always attract so much attention. The crowd always seems to know just how to move, to keep out of the way of flying punches and to let the fighters move around and have the space they need. Each second more and more people were running over to watch this latest playground attraction.

All of a sudden I got pushed from the side as Andrew came running and pushing past. As he parted the crowd in front I could see who was fighting, and realised it was two boys from our year. Andrew went straight up to the two boys with no fear of being hit himself. As the crowd quietened down to see what would happen next,

Andrew was able to make himself heard to the boys. One of the boys, Kenneth, was Andrew's friend and Brian, the other fighter, was in several of Andrew's classes. He pushed the two of them apart and spoke to them. I couldn't hear what he said, but it obviously meant something to the boys. They turned away from each other and picked up their school bags and went back to the rest of their friends. As the crowd realised the fight had ended they dispersed.

Andrew walked away with Kenneth, and the rest of his friends and the incident was over. Wow! It really made me wonder what Andrew had said to the boys to make such an impact. I know Andrew's not my fourteen year old Jesus reminder any more, but I'm sure his actions would have been just the kind of thing Jesus would have done. I bet, just like Andrew showed, he would be able to break up a fight between friends by the power of his words. That's quite a thought, to have the authority in your words that can stop actions.

We walked back into the school building to head up to our registration class. "See," said Anna, "there's always stuff going on with people at high school. Forget about Fiona. Bets on you have a fun filled afternoon!"

Chapter 15 - White Out

Wednesday afternoons begin with Biology and then finish with Maths, so I wasn't convinced by Anna's enthusiasm about a fun afternoon.

Today in Biology we're watching a DVD about worms. Mmmm... why do I like this subject so much?

The Biology room is set up with science benches, so it's not the best set up for watching the TV. Plus you sit on stools, so it's not so comfy when you're just sitting watching TV. As you can imagine the film was not exactly exciting. After five minutes Julie and I were looking at each other in complete and utter boredom.

Julie took a sheet of paper out of her folder and started writing something. She passed the sheet over. She'd started a game of knots and crosses. We played for five minutes then she switched to Hangman. After ten minutes of that she got bored. When the sheet of paper came back again she'd started off a conversation between two worms!

"You need to keep the conversation going," whispered Julie. I managed not to giggle out loud as I decided what the worms would say to each other next.

As the paper passed between us we got more and more into our worm conversation. So much so that we kind of lost track of what was happening in the classroom.

Before we realised it Mr Gibb was standing behind us.

"Rachel! Julie! What are you doing?" he shouted.

We both jumped at being caught.

"I'll see you both at the end of the class," he said, as he snatched the paper away from us.

As the class ended Julie and I walked over to Mr Gibb's desk. He handed us both a worksheet booklet.

"Well girls as you seem to be so keen on writing about worms you can complete these worksheets for the next biology class. DVDs are for your education. Not an optional part of class that you may either watch or ignore. I expect this is the last time I shall see such behaviour from either of you."

As we walked out of the class together we tried not to giggle. Mr Gibb is not the strictest of teachers. He's annoying but he's not fierce. So when he gives you into trouble it's difficult to take him seriously. But on the back of the Home Ec exercise it wasn't turning out to be the best of days. I would need to try and keep my head down in Maths and get some work done there.

I was a bit late getting to Maths, having been held back a few minutes by Mr Gibb. Everyone was already in their seats.

I had seen David and Fiona talking at lunch time and I could tell by the big grin on his face that he knew about the fish incident.

"Hey Anderson. Did you manage to eat all your lunch or did you drop it on the floor?" laughed David.

It was going to be a real trial to get through the class. I decided that the best approach was to concentrate on the maths problem at hand and try to ignore David. Of course that was easier said than done. When David was in a mood to annoy you, you just couldn't get away from him.

Mr Thomson started the class by explaining what we were going to be working through in our next chapter on Trigonometry. As usual it sounded okay when he talked about it, but I knew I would never be able to get the equations to work out when I tried it on my own. After speaking to us for half an hour, he set us a few examples to test our understanding.

Intent on trying to understand at least one aspect of Trig I set about with the first question. Things were going okay. I had managed to block out that David was sitting beside me. But then as I was writing in my jotter, trying to work out the solution, he started pushing my elbow and made me score across my jotter with my pen. Honestly he is so childish! Doesn't he realise that's the kind of thing that should be left at primary school?

I calmly took out my correction fluid and covered over the pen mark.

As I got back to working out the problem he pushed my elbow again. Again I calmly used the correction fluid.

I ignored him and got back to trying to solve the Trig problem, but he pushed my elbow again.

That's it! Enough is enough.

I turned round and threw the correction fluid over David's desk. The white liquid went all over his jotter, his text book, his pencil case and onto his shirt.

In a flash Mr Thomson was at our desks.

"That's enough both of you!" he yelled. "I want both of you out in the corridor right now."

I looked at him in shock. I couldn't believe it. First an exercise from Home Ec, then the Biology exercise and then being put outside the Maths class.

But worse was to come.

My face was burning red with embarrassment. As

we walked to the door everyone in the class was staring at us. We stood outside, looking away from each other, when all of a sudden the headmaster, Mr Pierce, walked round the corner. Oh no!

"You two! What are you doing standing there?" boomed Mr Pierce.

On hearing his voice Mr Thomson appeared at the classroom door. Mr Thomson didn't even mention the mess on the desk, just that we had been arguing and disrupting the class. Mr Pierce decided he would take both David and myself to his office as further punishment.

I couldn't believe what was happening. It was like a nightmare.

Mr Pierce is one of the scariest men I have ever met. Which I guess is a good quality for the headmaster of a large school. But at this moment in time I rather wished he wasn't quite so scary. Even hearing him shout at other kids makes me want to cry. I could feel the tears welling up inside me.

He took us up to his office and told us to sit in the waiting area outside of his office. I could tell my face had changed from the burning red of embarrassment to the ultra pale white of shock. But then something quite amazing and unexpected happened.

"I'm really sorry I bugged you and got you into trouble, Rachel," apologised David.

I looked at him in disbelief. I couldn't believe I was hearing those words come from David's lips. I knew I should say something back about it being okay, and it was my fault too, but I was in shock. I think the day had just been too much for me.

Mr Pierce called us both into his office.

"I can see from your records that neither of you are normally trouble makers. But you have to learn that you cannot disturb classes. It is not fair on the rest of the pupils in the class and it is not fair on the teacher."

"Yes Mr Pierce."

"At lunch time tomorrow I want you both here in my office where I will give you a punishment exercise to complete. In addition my secretary has prepared a letter for each of you, to tell your parents that you have been brought to my office because of unruly behaviour. These letters must be signed by your parents and brought back with you tomorrow. Is that clear?"

"Yes Mr Pierce."

"Now go back to your class and apologise to Mr Thomson."

We walked back to the class in silence.

Mr Pierce's theory on discipline is to be extra strict with "first time offenders" in the hope of scaring us witless so that we'll never get into trouble again. He goes over the top on minor crimes. One day when we were in the canteen eating lunch, a chip fell off of Anna's plate. Julie, out of some automatic reaction, flicked the chip off the table just as Mr Pierce walked into the canteen. Talk about bad timing. She was immediately marched off to Mr Pierce's office and had to stay there for the rest of the lunch break writing an essay on why it was impolite to flick chips onto the floor.

With just five minutes left of class Mr Thomson set us to work to tidy and clean David's desk. We both knew he was disappointed with us, and that he felt annoyed at Mr Pierce having been involved.

As the home time bell rang I felt a sense of dread at having to tell my parents what had happened. But before that was the dress rehearsal for the play. It was the most unenthusiastic I had felt for the play since I got the part. How could I possibly go up on stage and act when I felt so awful. I had just had the worst day ever, all I wanted to do was crawl under my duvet, not be the person up on stage.

Chapter 16 – Dress Rehearsal

The dress rehearsal started off well. I was even starting to enjoy myself and felt quite happy. But as we got to the final scene and my extra lines my mind went blank.

I had memorised my lines, I knew exactly what I was supposed to say. But my new lines had just disappeared from my memory. No matter how hard I tried I just couldn't remember what I was supposed to say.

I could remember the first lines, which had been the extent of my original part, but then I just stuttered and stammered as I tried to remember the next line. Miss Green was the prompter; she gave me the next line, and I repeated it, but then I just had no recollection of what the next line should be either. Once Miss Green realised that I had forgotten the rest of my lines, she stood up next to me and just read them out herself.

"I trust we can expect better than this on Friday," said Mrs Walsh.

"Yes, miss," I replied, although I felt anything but hopeful that I would be able to hold it together on Friday either.

As I looked round the hall and the stage I could see a mixture of reactions to my messing up.

The two actors whose lines I'd been given looked with annoyance at me. Fiona was gloating, no surprise there. David had a strange look on his face that was either sympathy or embarrassment for me, probably embarrassment. Claire definitely had a look of sympathy for me. And Mrs Walsh just looked fed up.

I couldn't wait to get out of the hall. I didn't even bother getting out of my stage clothes, I just grabbed my school uniform, and ran out of the hall. The last thing I could hear from the hall was the sound of Fiona's laughter, and I knew she was laughing at me.

As I walked home the tears streamed down my face, I didn't even care that people were looking at me. Let them look, they didn't know how rubbish my day had been. And now I had to go home and tell my mum and dad all about it, and about the punishment exercises I had been given. How could I possibly tell them about all this when they were still mad at me about Claire's party. I just hoped they wouldn't pull me out of the play, although after today's performance maybe that wouldn't be such a bad thing.

"How was school today?" shouted mum from the kitchen as she heard me come in.

"Okay," I replied as I grabbed a can of juice. "I'm just going up to my room to get on with some homework."

Mum eyed me suspiciously. I could tell she knew something was up. I'm never that quiet when I get in from school. I knew I was going to have to tell her about Home Ec, Biology and Maths. But I decided to wait until dad was home. That way I would only need to endure the telling off once rather than twice.

Using homework as a distraction from everything else that had gone on that day proved very useful. I got through all my work in record time, and with a lot more concentration than usual. Probably down to only doing homework and not multi-tasking it with watching TV or chatting on the internet.

After dinner I sat down with mum and dad and told them all about my day. The Home Ec and Biology incidents and arguing with David and being caught by Mr Pierce. Amazingly they were pretty cool with the whole thing and didn't go crazy at me. Parents are weird; they never respond the way you expect them to. They did however tell me that I had to stay in and was not allowed to go onto messenger, watch TV or use the phone.

I went to my room with a feeling of actually having my parents on my side. But I'm sure I heard them both laughing after I left them.

Although I was under a phone ban, I sent Anna a text to tell her how talking to mum and dad had gone. And that I was banned from the computer and phone calls. I did feel quite relieved at not being allowed to use the phone as I couldn't have faced the idea of speaking to anyone, even Anna.

I sat feeling sorry for myself. Happy to be left alone in my misery. I wanted to crawl into bed and hide under my duvet.

Anna sent me a text back immediately asking if I was okay. I told her I just wanted to go to sleep and I'd see her in the morning.

The next minute I got a text from Julie asking if I was okay. Anna and Julie had obviously been chatting together about the events of the day. Again I sent a text saying I was just going to sleep and I'd see her in the morning.

I didn't want to talk to anyone, but it was really nice to know that my friends were there for me, wanting to check that I was okay. I was comforted by their concern, but I just wanted to hide under my duvet.

Do you ever get the feeling of just wishing you could sort of disappear? That things would be easier for the world if you weren't around getting in the way of things. It was one of those nights for me.

I felt exhausted, but by 11:30pm I still couldn't get to sleep. My mind kept turning over and over all the events of the day. Wishing I'd reacted differently. Wishing Fiona or David or both had been off sick. Dreading the idea of being in Mr Pierce's office tomorrow. Embarrassment for messing up my lines in the play. Round and round and round the thoughts went. Driving me crazy. Keeping me from sleeping.

Out of either frustration or desperation I reached over to get my mp3 player. I scrolled through my artist listings to see who I would listen too. I chose my Simplicity album. It's full of instrumental pieces. I didn't think words would be helpful. I needed to calm down and find some peace. I didn't think Jesus would want to be with me, not with the mood I was in. But just in case he was still close by I had to try something.

Chapter 17 - The Office

Do you ever have one of those days when you wake up knowing that something is very wrong with your life? Knowing that something you did was wrong. And as you gradually come to full consciousness the reality of yesterday comes flooding back to your mind.

I really wanted to stay under my duvet. I didn't want to go to school. I didn't want to have to face anyone. I especially didn't want to have to sit in Mr Pierce's office with David.

And to top it all I had a big spot at the end of my nose! Why do spots head for the most obvious place on your face? Do you think Jesus ever had spots as a teenager? Kind of feels like one of those questions you're not supposed to ask. Although I guess it's probably more of a problem for us with all our fast food and chocolate. But Jesus must have gone through the whole teenage thing of changing hormones and stuff.

The walk to school was a painfully slow process. My thoughts bounced between wishing Anna was with me to dreading a lunch time in Mr Pierce's office.

The morning passed quickly enough. But in each class the only thing I could really think about was having to sit in the headmaster's office at lunch time. I'd never even been sent to his office before, and now I was going to have to spend a whole lunch break there!

As the lunch time bell rang the dread spread from the pit of my stomach through the whole of my body. I felt at a complete low in the What If Jesus was a teenager. I mean, how could I possibly imagine walking with Jesus and be going to the headmaster's office? I think that if Jesus was here he would be going to lunch with Anna right now, instead of being with me.

David was already standing outside the door as I walked to Mr Pierce's office.

"Hi," I said. Amazed I was able to speak a word from my dry mouth.

"Hey," he replied. He also seemed a lot quieter than his usual self.

The door opened and Mr Pierce ushered us into his office. As we walked into the office we both handed him the signed letters from our parents.

In his office was a big desk and in front of that were two individual desks. All along one side there were windows facing out onto the playground. Along another wall was a row of bookcases crammed full of books. Mr Pierce was both a History teacher and a Latin teacher before he became a headmaster, and from a quick glance it appeared that almost all the books were on his chosen subjects.

On each of the small desks there was a pad of paper and a thick history book.

"Sit down both of you. I want you to start copying the text from the books on your desks. I'll be back in half an hour to check on you. My secretary is just outside and will inform me if there are any problems with either of you." With that he left the office and went to the canteen, where he regularly checks that the pupils are behaving themselves over lunch.

"You know I really am sorry about yesterday," said David.

"David don't talk in here. We don't want to get in any more trouble."

But then I felt guilty, he had just apologised after all. Maybe the whole episode from yesterday would teach us to get over our usual stand offs.

"I'm sorry," I said. "You were just trying to be nice. I'm sure it's fine if we chat quietly. As long as we keep writing from these books. What's your book about?"

"The Industrial Revolution."

"Sounds like you win on the boring book scale. I've got a book about the Egyptians. It's quite interesting actually."

"What did your parents say about your punishments from yesterday?" asked David. I knew it. I knew he couldn't be nice to me for long. I tried my hardest to send a glaring look over in his direction. But I don't think I'm very good at the dramatic glances.

Instead of backing off David laughed. "Don't worry," he continued, "I'll be nice to you. I won't even mention again that you didn't just get into trouble in Maths, but also in Home Ec and Biology."

"How did you know about Biology?" I blurted out. "I'm glad to see my misfortunes are able to bring joy to others."

"Don't be too hard on yourself Anderson. We all have our off days. Yours was just a bit more intense than most."

Before I realised it I was saying, "But this isn't supposed to be happening to me. I'm supposed to be better this month not getting punishment exercises."

"What are you talking about?"

I'd started so I may as well continue. What did I have to lose? I told him about the What If Jesus was fourteen challenge. As I finished I expected him to laugh and make fun of me. But he sat silently. Before he could say anything else Mr Pierce walked in.

Mr Pierce checked on how much we'd both written. Then to our horror he sat down at his desk and started working. David and I exchanged glances, and then for the rest of the lunch break it was heads down and writing.

My conversation with David hadn't exactly been a "shout about Jesus from the roof top" thing. But somehow I'd ended up telling him about my belief in Jesus. I suddenly felt like Jesus was there. I felt myself sink into Jesus' peace and enjoyed him being there. What do you know? Jesus was in the headmaster's office after all!

The bell rang to signal the end of lunch break. Mr Pierce checked how much writing we'd both achieved and then dismissed us with a warning to behave in class.

As we stepped out of his office we both sighed a huge sigh of relief. We walked along to our registration classes together.

"I couldn't believe he stayed in the office with us," I said.

"I know. I was enjoying our time until then," replied David.

I laughed, not really sure if he was trying to imply something there or not.

"You looking forward to tomorrow's Geography trip?" asked David.

"Yeah. It'll be great to get out of school for the day. This hasn't exactly been my best week ever."

"I did notice," replied David. "I was the one on the receiving end!"

"Don't pretend to be innocent, David. You give as

good as you get."

David laughed. He didn't even have another come back line. Had I actually managed to silence his sarcasm? Just in time, before he had a chance to think of anything else to say, we reached our registration classes.

"See you in Maths later," called David as he went into his registration class.

I made my way to registration feeling peaceful and happy. I could almost feel Jesus walking along the corridor beside me. And that's when the whole "*What If* Jesus was fourteen" challenge clicked. Jesus is my friend. I don't need to try and be perfect to be Jesus' friend. After all, he's just been in the headmaster's office with me. Not because, like me, he had to be there, but because he wanted to be with me and support me. Just as Anna sticks by me no matter what, so does Jesus. Can't quite imagine why he'd want me as his friend, but I have the feeling that he does.

As I walked into class Anna and Julie came over to me. They had such concerned looks on their faces. Friends are a great thing to have.

"It's fine," I smiled to them both. "It went okay. Mr Pierce was in the office for a bit. And when he wasn't, David and I chatted."

They both looked a bit confused as to why David and I had been chatting. It made me smile to see them try and make sense of my comment.

Chapter 18 – Geography Field Trip

The next day I woke up to a beautiful sunny morning. I felt happy. I was full of enthusiasm for the field trip and full of anticipation for the school play. It was perfect weather for the Geography field trip day. And great timing to be getting out of school for the day. Even though yesterday went pretty well, it would still be good to get out and about and have a break from classroom life.

One of my Friday classes is Music. I am completely tone deaf, so never do very well in Music class. At the moment we're getting taught guitar. I used to go to guitar lessons at church. One of our worship leaders went by the belief that it was every Christian's responsibility to be able to play guitar. And from that mindset she started up kids' guitar lessons. I proved her very wrong in her theory. I was the worst person at guitar she'd ever come across. Thankfully Jesus holds no such requirements for us! But now I'm getting guitar at school, and even I will admit that there has been no improvement in my musical ability whatsoever.

After registration I went to the Geography department with Anna. There were twelve of us going out, and two teachers, Mr Niel and Mr James. Mr Niel had stressed time and time again that we were to wear practical clothing for the trip, but four of the girls in the group, including Fiona, were wearing their new jeans and t-shirts. More designed for sunny days rather than cool October field trips. Geography field trips involve tramping through muddy fields and streams, so Mr Niel always makes a big deal with everyone about wearing older clothes and wellie boots.

"You girls!" shouted Mr Niel, drawing everyone's attention to the fashionable crowd.

"I want all of you to go down to the janitor's office and ask for lost property sweaters. There is no way you can go out without a sweater. I will not be responsible for anyone getting hypothermia"

The girls walked off grumbling. But Mr Niel had a smile on his face. I'm sure he must find it hilarious that people can be so fashion conscious on a Geography field trip.

Once the girls came back we all headed to the school mini bus.

"Does anyone get travel sick?" asked Mr Niel.

No one replied. I guess experience has taught him that in a mini bus of school kids there's bound to be someone who will start to feel sick at some point in the journey. Especially when you're going along winding country roads to get to a river source.

"Okay then, everyone in."

Anna and I sat together near the front. We were both really looking forward to the trip.

After half an hour we left the main roads and headed up into the hills. The drive was beautiful. All you could see were hills and trees, not a school building in sight.

"It used to all be open space up here," explained Mr Niel. "But then about twenty years ago the Forestry Commission started planting trees. Remember this for next term. We'll be going on to talk about forestry then."

The road started getting narrower. Then it became a single track road with passing places. After ten minutes of the winding road even I was beginning to feel a bit nauseous, and I never get car sick. Mr Niel was driving and Mr James was sitting beside him up front. The two of them were chattering away about Geography stuff, unaware that in the back of the bus the class was getting quieter and quieter.

"STOP!" came a shout from the back of the bus. "I'm going to be sick."

It was David. His face had turned ashen white.

Mr Niel pulled the bus over to the side of the road. He jumped out and ran round to the back of the bus to open the door. He was just in time. David got out the bus and immediately started being sick. Unfortunately, for Mr Niel, his shoes were the recipient of most of it! But at least he had his wellington boots to change into.

Once David had finished being sick Mr Niel moved him to the front seat. As David climbed back into the mini bus the other boys all started laughing at him and made fun of him. I guess for boys travel sickness goes against the whole macho thing. Although I do think it was a bit of bad luck for David. It was a bit of a close call as to who was going to be sick first.

After another ten minutes Mr Niel pulled the mini bus over to the side of the road and we all got out. We followed Mr Niel and Mr James as they led us to a point near the river source. They handed out worksheets and clipboards and told us the assignments we had for the morning. The plan for the day was to have a general look at the path the river had taken, specifically looking at where it starts and where it ends.

"Okay everyone," shouted Mr Niel. "Get into pairs.

We'll be spending about an hour up here looking at features of the river source. Then we'll have a break for lunch. After lunch we'll head back to the bus and drive downstream to study the lower region of the river. We'll be spending about an hour down there before heading back to school."

I love Geography field trips and finding out stuff about how nature works and how you can better understand the world around you. The scenery around us was just gorgeous, the hills, the river, the trees, it all looked amazing. I'm so grateful to live in a country where there is so much beauty. Jesus must have loved nature. He must have noticed so much of the beauty, the complexity and the wonder of what was around him.

"How great is this?" said Anna. "A whole day out of school. I know we haven't done any work yet, but it does feel like a day off."

"I know. A reward for a rough week." I replied.

Anna gave me one of her looks. "Come on, Rachel! It's not been that bad."

"I guess. Just not as good as I hoped it was going to be."

We worked in pairs for just over an hour then we were all called together to have lunch.

"You okay?" I asked David as he sat down to eat his lunch.

"I'm fine," he said. "Just not too keen on those little roads."

I gave him a smile as I turned round to go and sit beside Anna.

Anna gave me a look. The kind of look that made it clear she was expecting me to do some explaining.

"I know," I said. "A week ago I would never have uttered a civil word to David. And now, having spent time in Mr Pierce's office together, we've been able to get past the enemy thing to being nice to each other."

Anna said little in reply. But I could tell there were a lot of thoughts running through her mind. Thoughts she decided to keep to herself for the time being.

Mr Niel and Mr James spent lunch time talking about adventures they'd had going hill walking. As teachers go these two guys are pretty funny. They had us laughing and wishing we were going off for a weekend hill walking.

Just as we were finishing up with lunch David came over to sit beside Anna and me. Now I may have been willing to send a civil word David's way. But here was the sign of how much more confident David is than me. He was able to just walk right over and sit down for a chat. I could see Fiona looking over. Annoyance and curiosity written all over her face.

David was full of conversation and questions - How had we got on with our worksheet? What did we think of Mr Niel? What were we up to at the weekend? Of course he did do a lot of talking about himself, which did get a bit annoying. But I guess it was better than the usual arguing.

"Everyone back to the bus now," shouted Mr Niel.

As we all headed back to the bus David gently caught the side of my arm. "Thanks for asking if I was okay this morning. Can't believe you of all people were the only one to check I was okay."

Oh no! I could feel my face burning red. I wasn't prepared for the butterflies in my stomach at David's words and touch. It seemed all a guy had to do was speak to me and I felt attracted to him. Think I preferred the feeling of wanting to throw things at him!

Chapter 19 - Splash

We all got back into the bus and went further down river. I looked out of the window and thought about David. I wondered again about Andrew's comments about David's life not being as easy as he made out. Not for the first time I wondered what the issues were and how David was able to rise above it all at school and be a cool guy. Could his life really be tough, or was Andrew blowing things out of proportion?

I also considered my feelings towards David. How could I go from one extreme to the other so quickly with him. Anna would probably just tell me I was over complicating everything again, and maybe I was. I was beginning to think that maybe the result of the teenage Jesus challenge was to think again about friendships. Instead of complicating or reading too much into these new feelings for David, maybe I should just grow up and see him as a friend.

Mr Niel parked the mini bus at our afternoon location. At this lower part of the river the ground was fairly flat and the river was meandering through the landscape. Late summer had been dry, so the river was quite shallow, but you got the general idea of the river phase from the full breadth of the river bed.

Mr Niel led us to a footbridge that crossed the river. He instructed half of the group to cross to the other side, while the rest of us were to stay where we were.

As we were working through our exercises, I looked over and saw Fiona and her friend Sarah working together. Fiona was getting closer and closer to the river bank as she took notes of the river pattern. Mr Niel had warned us about the banks at this meandering stage of the river, explaining to us that the river can undercut the bank. So what may seem like a safe place to stand isn't. From where we were working I could see that Fiona was getting closer to an overhanging part of the bank, with the river flowing underneath it.

"Don't stand there, Fiona!" I shouted over.

But as usual she ignored me. She took one more step forward and...

SPLASH!

As the overhang collapsed under Fiona's weight, she fell into the river, bum first. Thankfully the river wasn't as full as it should have been for the time of year, so there was no fear of her drowning. She just had to cope with getting soaked. But for Fiona, sitting soaking wet in a river, was probably as traumatic as drowning.

The loud splash, and the girlie screams from Fiona and her friends, brought the rest of the group running over to see what was happening. As you can imagine the boys all found the scene totally hilarious. They all pointed and laughed. For the most part the other girls weren't saying too much. Each one thankful it had happened to Fiona and not them. Mr Niel was the last to arrive at the scene.

This was just the kind of thing that Mr Niel's sarcastic sense of humour loved.

"Fiona, can you leave the baths for home if you don't mind!" This of course sent the boys into a fresh fit of laughter and pointing.

Fiona's shocked screams now turned to tears. Everyone had come over to look, but no one thought to help her out.

The river was shallow enough for me to wade in with my boots on.

"Come on," I called over to her, "I'll help you out."

She looked over at me with a look combining surprise, embarrassment and resentment. I was probably the last one in the group she wanted help from. But I was the closest person to be able to help. Most of the group were on her side of the bank, and it was too risky to try and get her from there, where she had fallen in was now a dirt slide. And on either side of that there was more overhanging embankment.

"Thanks." Was all she said as she took my hand of help. Her voice was flat. I guess it was probably one of those incidents where she just wanted the ground to open up and swallow her. I knew what that felt like. Instead she had half a class standing around her, seeing it all.

As I helped her out, all the others on the opposite side of the river made their way over the bridge to join us.

"I've got a change of clothes you can borrow," I offered.

My mum always makes me pack extra stuff for these kind of outings - I think she expects me to be the one getting into problems.

"Thanks." Again the short, flat response to my help. Honestly, you would think she could have been a little more grateful! I realised that my attitude towards Fiona had been slowly changing over the last few weeks. A couple of months ago I would have been laughing at Fiona's misfortunes, but I didn't want to laugh at her now. I felt sorry for her and genuinely wanted to help her. But I also realised just because my attitude towards her had changed, it didn't mean that she had changed her opinion about me.

As we walked back towards the bus Fiona shot me one of her looks. It's the look she's perfected over the years. The look that lets you know she has a very low opinion of you, that as far as she is concerned you'll always be on the outside looking in, never part of her crowd. How do you get yourself over that kind of a rejection, especially when you're helping the person? It made me feel like there was no point in trying to reach out and make new friends.

The bus journey back to school provided me with some time to think over recent events. Specifically David and Fiona. A few weeks ago I would have said that there was no way I would ever be friends with either of them, that they moved in very different circles than I did. But just a few weeks on and how much has changed. I'm sure David and I will still have our times of arguing, especially in Maths, but it really does feel like we've turned a corner, and I can even imagine us being friends. He felt bad for pushing me too far in Maths, and through that we've both changed. Thinking about Jesus as a teenager and the conversation I'd had with Andrew about David had both helped to change my attitude to him.

And then there's Fiona. From almost the same starting point as with David, and yet how different are the outcomes. After everything I've done for Fiona today she still wants to keep me at arm's length, and refuses any steps towards a friendship. It's not that I'm particularly looking to become Fiona's friend, I'm just amazed at how negative she still is towards me. I've reached out to her but friendship only works if it goes both ways. I realised my feelings were hurt by her reaction to me, and that hurt just wanted to say "who cares about Fiona?".

Chapter 20 – Missing

By the time we got back to school I felt really tired. Nerves were starting to get the better of me. After my poor performance at the dress rehearsal I was starting to feel really worried. It had been a relief to be out of school today, but after Fiona's reaction I was feeling all confused and down again.

We had arrived back at school a few minutes before the home time bell rang.

"How are you feeling?" asked Anna.

"Nervous."

"You'll be great. Don't worry about what happened on Wednesday. That was just last minute nerves on top of a difficult day. Mrs Walsh would never have given you those extra lines if she didn't think you were capable of the performance."

Anna's words were working, I was starting to feel a bit calmer. She was right, I could do this. The bell rang to signal the end of the school day. The doors burst open and suddenly there were kids everywhere, hurrying out of school to get to their weekends. I saw some of the familiar faces from the play heading over towards the main hall.

"I better go in and make sure everything is okay. See you later at the show."

"Enjoy it Rachel, you'll be fab."

And with her usual smile and wave Anna headed off towards the school gate.

Mrs Walsh was waiting for us all as we arrived at the hall.

"Okay everyone; our schedule for this afternoon is as follows. I've got a few general things I need to go through with you all about the play: such as stage positioning and scene endings. I will also need to speak to a few of you individually about your delivery. Then we'll have something to eat. After that you can all get changed into your costumes."

Oh no; our costumes! I had forgotten to bring my costume back to school with me. How could I have been so forgetful? Normally I would have left it at school. But I had been so upset on Wednesday after my terrible performance that I had just run from the hall still in my Jemma outfit. And because it had always been left at school before then, I had completely forgotten about bringing it back.

What could I do?

If I told Mrs Walsh she would go crazy at me, especially after I'd messed up my lines. I could feel the panic rise in me again. That old familiar feeling of messing up. I started pacing around trying to think of what to do. At that moment Andrew walked into the hall.

"Hi Rachel," he said.

"What?" was the only reply I could manage, having hardly registered that he'd even spoken to me.

"You okay?" he asked, in a very concerned voice.

"Oh Andrew, you're never going to believe what I've done." And then I told him that I'd just realised I'd left my costume at home.

"Calm down Rachel. We'll get it here on time. Why

don't you call Anna and ask her if she can go and get it and bring it straight back to school for you?"

I burst out laughing, which made Andrew look even more concerned. "Andrew, you're brilliant. That's a great idea. And don't worry, I'm only laughing because that's just the kind of thing Anna would suggest too. Then she'd laugh at me for over complicating things, instead of looking for the simple solution. Thanks. I'll go out and give her a call right now."

"I'll wait with you in case there is any problem. If she can't help I could always go and get it for you. I don't think anyone would notice if I popped out for a bit."

I called Anna and she said that she would be able to help out straight away. She promised she'd get back to the school as soon as possible, and that she'd send me a text to let me know when she arrived with my Jemma clothes.

I felt such a sense of relief, now I just had to hope that Mrs Walsh wouldn't be asking any of us to get into our costumes before Anna arrived. Even though the disaster had now blown over, Andrew stayed beside me and chatted to me a bit more. We chatted about our week, well mostly about my week, and all the trouble I'd gotten into. I also told him about Thursday being a day of clarity for me. That I began to realise that Jesus is here as a friend for us. Andrew laughed as I described the situation to him, but he also had a reassuring smile.

Andrew and Anna are really quite similar in a lot of ways. It's been really nice getting to know him a bit more these last few weeks, even if it did come about from my grand scheme back firing. Both of them have a quiet confidence about them that can really help put you at ease, and reassure you that you are a friend. Anna is much more outgoing than Andrew, but deep down I think they are similar.

As I was thinking about how nice it was to have Andrew as a friend, David came over to us.

"So Anderson, you all ready for your big performance?"

"Yeah, getting there. Just need to steady my nerves a bit then I should be okay."

"Don't worry about having some nerves," said Andrew, "after all, nerves are supposed to help you give an amazing performance. It gives you an adrenalin rush, and puts you on edge, gets you really thinking and really performing."

David looked at Andrew, and then back at me as I laughed at his words of encouragement. He had a strange look on his face that was hard to read. I decided to change the subject.

"So how you feeling David? Did you manage the rest of the journey okay?"

He laughed, but before we could say any more Mrs Walsh arrived in the hall and ordered us all to the stage area. She ran through a couple of last minute points, mostly about positionings and scene starts and endings. Thankfully she didn't get me to go through my lines again.

She then told us to have something to eat, and in half an hour we were all to start getting into our costumes. I still hadn't heard anything from Anna, and I was starting to feel a bit nervous, something must have delayed her. I could feel the worry start to creep up from my stomach. Andrew must have detected my worry and came over to where I was sitting.

"Have you still not heard back from Anna?"

"No, I thought she would have been here by now. I tried to call her, but it's just going to her voice mail."

"Try not to worry, I'm sure it'll be fine. Why don't you give me her number and then I can keep trying to call her. I'll head over to yours to see if I can find her, see if she needs any help. Then I can bring your costume back for you. I don't need to get changed or anything, so I've got more time than you to sort this out."

"Andrew, that's so nice. Thank you, that would be a big help."

As Andrew took Anna's number I could see David looking over. There was a look of more than just curiosity on his face. As Andrew reached the doors of the hall David caught up with him. They spoke briefly, Andrew nodded and then they left the hall together. Why was David going with him?

As I watched them leaving, Claire came over to where I was sitting.

"How you feeling?" she asked.

"Nervous. After my forgotten lines at the dress rehearsal I'm a bit worried about tonight."

"Don't worry about it, you'll be fine. We all have off days, yours is now out of the way so you can put in a great performance tonight."

"So do you still suffer from stage fright?" I asked, changing the focus from me to her.

"Most times, but that can be a good thing. It helps to keep you sharp and focused." But then she switched back to me again. "I heard what happened after the party, about getting caught by your dad. That's too bad."

I felt my face flush red with the embarrassment of Claire knowing about my deception. But it also made me wonder why everyone else always seemed to know about what was going on in my life.

"Well I hope you had a good time at the party that more than made up for being caught," she said.

I just laughed. It was easier than trying to explain how much guilt I'd felt all weekend because of it.

"Anyway, I just wanted to say have a great time tonight. Relax and enjoy it, Rachel. You've got a great acting talent, so enjoy it. I know you'll be brill." She gave me a big hug and then walked off. I was so grateful for Claire, and for the friendship that had built up over the last few weeks. Fiona may appear to be a lost cause, but Claire more than makes up for it. I had loved getting to know her over the course of the play. It really was worth being open to new friendships, you just never knew what it would bring.

"Okay everyone, back stage, time to get into your costumes," called out Mrs Walsh.

Oh no, where were those guys? I wasn't going to be able to hide my lack of costume much longer. I took out my phone to check for any missed calls or messages, but there wasn't anything.

I got up and started to walk over to the door, I decided I would just pop out of the hall and try phoning Anna to see what was going on. But as I was approaching the door Andrew and David burst through, both of them looking a bit out of breath. David was carrying a bag with my costume. I was so relieved to see it.

"Sorry for the delay," said Andrew breathing heavily, "your parents weren't in when Anna got to your house, and she had to wait a bit."

"Thanks so much you guys. Where's Anna?"

"She'll be here for the show. Once we met up with her she went back to her house to get something to eat before coming to the show."

With gratitude, I took my costume from David, as I did so I got an electric shock from him. I looked at him, expecting some witty remark, instead he looked back at me with an intense look in his eyes, maybe it was due to all the running about he had just been doing.

The excitement of my missing costume had helped to distract me, but now I felt my body was overflowing with adrenaline. I had to gather myself back together and focus on my part. As I finished getting ready my phone buzzed with a received text. I didn't recognise the number displayed on the screen. I opened the text "u r gr8, b a star 2nite, David".

I laughed out loud. How else could I react after all the crazy stuff that had been going on over the past few weeks. David really was a difficult person to read. Maybe Andrew was right about the difficult background. In Mr Pierce's office he had seemed more real, more approachable. But with an audience he was different, I always thought it was confidence, but maybe it was just a facade. Still there was no audience with a text message, just sender and receiver. Was his message just one of friendship? Or *What If* it implied more?

Chapter 21 – The School Play

"Five minutes everyone," called Mrs Walsh. It was time to put everything else out of my head except the play. I said a prayer to calm myself down and went to stand next to the stage entrance.

The first half of the play went really well; you could tell that there were a few jitters amongst the performers, but they soon calmed down, and everyone was really getting into their parts and performing well. Things continued to go well during the second half, and then it was time for my closing lines.

""What If...?" Just two little words, but two little words that can change the world!

The Scientist asks "What If?" and a new medicine is discovered.
The Inventor asks "What If?" and a new product is presented to the world.
The Politician asks "What If?" and a country's government is improved.

But what happens when the teenager asks "What If?"

For the teenager life holds so many possibilities, so many
What Ifs.
What Ifs can be positive or negative
What If trying something new fails or
What If trying something new opens amazing new windows
of opportunity?

What Ifs can be a gamble
What If a friendship is lost
What If a friendship is won
What If a friendship is strengthened?

To ask What If is the easy part
To ignore the What If can lead to regret
So the next time you're asked "What If?"
What will you do?"

As the hall erupted into rapturous applause I couldn't help
but feel proud. The cast all came together and we gave our
bows, Claire was presented with some beautiful flowers, as
was Mrs Walsh.

As I looked round the stage I saw Claire, beaming
with delight at yet another fantastic performance. And over
in the band corner I could see Andrew and David as they
took their bows for the band performance, both of them
with smiles on their faces. I smiled to myself, what would
be in store for me now that I had guy friends? I was
looking forward to this new experience in my life. And as I
caught a glimpse of Fiona I could see even she was smiling,
maybe this time round she had rejected my friendship, but
who knows what the future holds.

From my vantage point on stage I was able to see
Anna and Julie sitting in the audience, close enough to the
front for me to be able to see them before the glow of the

stage lights faded into the audience. Both of them were looking at me, looking so pleased for me, and clapping so hard. I gave them a big smile, and mouthed thank you to them. They really are the best friends in the world. As I stood basking in the applause I could feel that Jesus was beside me too, and now I know I don't need to be perfect for him, I just need to be his friend. My best friends and my new friends all close by me.

As I enjoyed the moment I wondered what adventures the next *What If* would bring?

--The End--

Have you read Why Not?

Why Not? is the follow up to What If?. Continuing the story of Andrew, Anna, David and Rachel, taking place a few months after What If?

Why Not?

ISBN-978-0-9570039-3-4

Why Not…? Just two little words. Two little words that can strike fear or bring encouragement depending on who is asking.

Fourteen-year-old Andrew McFarlane thinks of himself as just average, especially now he is spending more time with the popular group at school. Andrew needs to make decisions on subject choices, girlfriends, friendships and faith, but are the people around him looking out for their own interests or his?

Why not read Andrew's story and find out?

Keep In Touch

Check out my website for further information and my online shop. Why not sign up to receive regular newsletters?

www.carolinejohnston.co.uk

Follow me on social media for updates and news:

www.facebook.com/carolinejohnstonauthor

www.twitter.com/author_caroline

www.instagram.com/carolinej_author